BUNNY MISFIT

THE MISFITS #3

EVE LANGLAIS

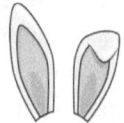

Copyright © 2018 Eve Langlais

Cover Art © 2018 Dreams2Media

Produced in Canada

Published by Eve Langlais

http://www.EveLanglais.com

eBook ISBN: 978 177384 0604

Print ISBN: 978 177384 0611

This book is a work of fiction and the characters, events and dialogue found within the story are of the author's imagination and are not to be construed as real. Any resemblance to actual events or persons, either living or deceased, is completely coincidental.

No part of this book may be reproduced or shared in any form or by any means, electronic or mechanical, including but not limited to digital copying, file sharing, audio recording, email and printing without permission in writing from the author.

PROLOGUE

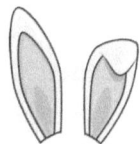

I SEEMED so normal when I was born.

Ten fingers and toes? Check.

Perfect skin, not a blemish to be seen.

As I grew, I was the apple of my parents' eyes. Not the smartest kid in class, or the most agile—I had two left feet and tripped over them often—but I definitely earned the trophy for the cutest girl in school. Apparently, my smile could make anyone's day brighter.

I had friends. Tons of them. Being popular came naturally to me, as did laughter.

Posters of the latest boy bands plastered my walls. My closet bulged with the trendiest clothes.

As a pack princess, I had it all. And by pack, I mean werewolf. My daddy was the alpha, the leader of us all, which made him the biggest and meanest of all the wolves around. Except with me. Daddy loved his little girl.

My mother was a bitch, which wasn't the nasty word you'd assume. It just meant that, like my daddy, she acted as top dog among the women. None proved stronger than her. None more assertive.

My parents had problems conceiving and needed the help of some fertility doctors and drugs. They only managed to have one child: me. The best of the best in one adorable body with curly blonde hair, a quick giggle, and a dimple in both cheeks. It should be noted I didn't resemble either of my parents.

Mother claimed I took after her side, Great-Great-Grandma June, as a matter of fact. I'd seen a portrait. The comparison didn't flatter. Father seemed to think the blonde came from his great-grandpa's philandering.

Anyhow, all this to say my life was perfect. I was perfect. And at sixteen—later than most—I finally got my period. Now I'd bled—more than a normal person should, surely, and I wasn't entirely reassured I wouldn't die as Mother claimed. Which might be too much information, but in a wolf pack, it was serious business. Because, for females, the onset of puberty, namely our menses, and the full moon after, kicked our genes into gear. In other words, I would now be able to shift.

I still remember sitting in the backyard—over an acre of lush green grass that mother tended with an eagle eye for weeds. The far edge of the yard edged by a forest. Protected parklands, also known as my playground. I lived with people who didn't believe in children being indoors or over protected with toys so safe they bored. My generation was encouraged to run wild in the forest. To climb trees and hang upside down from branches.

Sure, we broke a few bones when we fell. But we were fit. Strong. Adventurous. Everything a wolf-in-training should be. And finally, after years of waiting, it was my turn to roam the woods on four legs, just like my mom and dad and everyone who came before me.

I fidgeted on the grass with the other pups about to move from child to adult. Seven of us for that full moon. Janie Whittacker, being the youngest at twelve. She developed super early.

We wore only thin robes, nothing else, which meant we giggled a lot. The movies made it seem like werewolves and shapeshifters were totally into the nudity thing. False. Human skin was too naked. In animal form, at least we wore fur. I couldn't wait to see mine. Mother promised she'd get a picture. We were both curious to see if my blonde coloring would stick through the shift.

There was much blushing and shuffling of feet as we waited for the moon's rays to come out of hiding. The big ol' ball of green cheese teased us from behind a cloud. The tingle of its presence made my skin itch.

Feeling someone's gaze on me, I lifted my head and saw Derek, high school hottie, two years ahead of me and recently broken up with his girlfriend.

He winked.

I think I might have died a bit inside. Happiness killed. Who knew?

Anticipation boiled, and nerves grew taut as the clouds taunted us by refusing to move. When the moon did finally emerge, there was a collective sigh.

My mother's hand briefly brushed my hair as she said, "Don't be afraid." Whereas Father clapped my shoulder and said, "Go for the jugular if you want a quick kill." And by that he meant prey.

Because most junior wolves went wild the first few times they shifted. Lost their humanity and let primal instinct take over. I tried not to think about the killing part. I liked my steak well-cooked, if at all. Personally, I would have been vegan if my parents would allow it.

I took a deep breath. My hands fell to my sides, and I craned my face into the moonlight, letting it bathe my skin, starting a chain reaction in my cells as my wolf side bubbled to the surface.

It didn't hurt.

At first.

More like it tickled and the sparse hair on my body stood on end. The tickle turned to a burning sensation, as if someone took a hot brand to my skin, which, as you can imagine, caused pain. Extreme pain as bones—I preferred not to think about the fact it was my body—cracked and reshaped.

I did my best to hold the cries in. Not everyone succeeded. Moans, screams, and whimpers. I did my best not to add to the symphony. After all, everyone was watching—including Derek.

It lasted forever, which was to say less than a minute. An eternity when pain was involved. But the agony did at one point fade and I felt good. Alert. My senses enhanced, especially that of smell. Who knew there were so many flavors to be tasted in one breath?

I didn't realize at first something was wrong.

Really, really wrong.

Not until I heard the first gasp. "What is *that*?"

Followed by my mother's sobbing. Why was she crying? Had something bad happened?

Only then did I peer down at myself, wondering if I'd gotten crappy coloring like cousin Jeremiah or maybe a stunted tail like Aunt Posy.

The white paws lacking claws confused me. Which led to my nose twitching. Something sniffed me, a big hairy beast that jangled my nerves, and I squeaked. Quite literally.

It wasn't until someone said, "Did Claire just turn into a bunny?" that I realized just how horribly things had gone.

And then they got worse.

See, I'd shifted among wolves. Six new ones, who

got one whiff of yummy rabbit meat and...

Ever heard the announcer say, "And they're off!"

Understatement.

I bolted like a bunny with six hungry wolves on my tail.

I spent that entire first night running. Hiding. Burrowing. Eating the carrot—which was freaking delicious—I stole from a yard.

By the time dawn hit and I collapsed, a naked teenage girl in a pile of leaves, I was a shaking mess.

Oh my gawd. What is wrong with me? I cried at the injustice of it all. The shame.

It didn't help that it was Derek who found me. Fully dressed, I might add, leaving me at a distinct disadvantage.

He knelt beside me and offered me a robe. Knees tucked to my chest, and cheeks hotter than the waffle maker, I couldn't meet his gaze.

"You okay?" he asked.

"Yeah," I lied. How could I tell the hottest guy in school I was not okay? As a matter of fact, I'd never be okay.

Especially since after the floppy ear incident no one would really talk to me about it—unless it was to offer me carrots, thinking they were so funny. People avoided me at school. Whispered about me when I walked by. My friends ditched me. No one wanted to be seen with the freak.

The pack doctor I went to see had no answer as

to why I wasn't a wolf. No one could explain why I transformed into a never-before-seen rabbit.

As for my parents, to my face, they were supportive. Loving. But it was a sham. They fought behind closed doors. With my big ears, I heard every word. My father booming, "Is she even mine?"

My mother yelling back, "Of course she is. This is probably your fault. Your grandfather never did say who birthed your dad."

And on it went. To my face, I got platitudes. "Don't worry, honey. These things happen."

No, they didn't. I was a freak.

An oddity.

Prey among predators.

The next full moon, I wanted to hide away from everyone. Too embarrassed to be seen. But my dad insisted I try again. "Maybe it was just a fluke. Try thinking carnivorous thoughts when the moon hits you."

Despite it turning my stomach, I tried to imagine a big juicy steak with a side of buttered carrots. Next thing I knew I was running across the yard, the baying of wolves behind me.

My little heart beat so fast I thought it would explode. Especially since, this time, the wolves cornered me, forming a furry circle that wouldn't let me escape. In the distance, I heard baying, even recognized the warning in it. My dad was racing to my rescue.

But these young pups weren't listening. Terror froze me in place as their jaws snapped and slavered. I shook under gazes wild with the hunt.

I don't want to die.

The last thing I recalled, I closed my eyes because I didn't want to watch them eat me. Uncontrollable fear meant I whimpered and panted, my whiskers twitching, wishing I was bigger and stronger and...

Next time I blinked my eyes open, I was lying naked on the ground, still in the woods, covered in blood. None of it mine. I knew this by the taste it left on my tongue. But what really made me gag? The torn wolf ear on the ground beside me.

What did I do? My stomach heaved, and I retched, eyes closed as my body expelled things I preferred not to see. Chunky, gross things.

In the distance, I heard voices calling. But I didn't answer.

I didn't want anyone to find me, especially since I didn't know what had happened or how much trouble I might be in.

I can claim it was self-defense.

No one would blame me for protecting myself. The thing was I shouldn't have to. If one thing became certain in that moment, it was the fact I didn't belong with the pack anymore. At sixteen, with not even any clothes on my back, I ran away from home.

CHAPTER 1

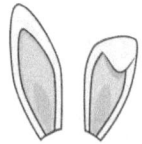

"Like hell is she leaving home." This from Lana, who reigned like a queen on the couch, her feet soaking in a tub of briny water. Her green hair was pulled back in a ponytail, and her summer dress hiked up over her knees. "If anyone goes, it should be me."

"You are not going anywhere," declared her mate, Jory, a strapping Viking who seemed to think forbidding Lana anything was a bright idea.

"I'm pregnant, not an invalid," Lana snarled, her voice reaching a pitch that made me wince even though it wasn't directed at me.

My head bounced to Jory for his reply. "You need to take it easy. The doctor said so."

"Only because he's a moron," she snapped. "Did you know he told me I should stop taking baths because showers are healthier? As if. He's lucky I didn't burst his eardrums for that stupidity."

No kidding, given Lana's mermaid side needed the immersion in water to remain hydrated.

"If you don't like him, then we'll get a new doctor. Maybe a woman doctor. What about Anya?" Jory suggested.

"Anya is a bloodthirsty Valkyrie whose claim to medical skill is stitching up your dumb ass when you play war with your Viking brothers." Lana sneered, her pregnancy hormones in full swing.

"Not true. I once saw Anya help another Valkyrie birth a babe on the battlefield. The mother recovered so quickly she fought with the child tucked into her tunic."

"I don't think so," shrieked Lana, causing the glass to rumble.

My neck was getting a great workout, but this really had to stop. "Lana, you're keeping your doctor. He's the best one around." Not to mention, he was slightly deaf so not as susceptible to Lana's mood swings. "As to the reconnaissance mission, I'm going, and that's final."

No way was I going to be talked out of the most epic adventure ever!

Seriously. This was going to be so much fun. Dangerous, too, which made my nose twitch, but my therapist said I needed to work on conquering my fear of...well...just about everything.

This mission was perfect for me. We—as in the misfit crew comprised of Beth, Lana, and me—

recently found out that Lana was the result of some sea god and a siren getting together. If you were thinking, oh how cute, they fell in love, you'd only be partially right. Apparently, Neptune and Bella disappeared over twenty years ago. People assumed they ran off together since theirs was a forbidden love, but it recently came to light they might have been kidnapped and used by human scientists in a breeding program.

Lana was the result. Half mermaid, half siren, total badass, and my best friend. My very pregnant best friend, who was less than impressed with her condition. Who knew that being impregnated by a demi-god would result in a shortened gestation? Lana was not happy about that part. Especially since her pregnancy was considered high risk. The doctor had ordered bed rest.

With Lana taken out of commission, it meant she couldn't follow the tip we'd gotten on a possible location for her parents.

"Why do you get to go and not me?" Lana whined. "This is my family we're talking about."

Even Beth, a very rare Nephilim, a demon and angel mix, the third BFF in this triumvirate, wasn't on her side. "Use your head for something more than a hat rack. Do you really think your mom and dad would want you to put that little tadpole in your belly nest in danger?"

"Maybe if your lazy boyfriend would snap his

fingers and do something useful, we wouldn't be having this discussion," huffed Lana.

Gene, a veritable genie and Beth's consort, shook his bald head. "I've told you before, the Rockies are off-limits. I can't teleport anywhere around there. There's something in those mountains that blocks magical travel. The closest I can get is Calgary."

Lana pouted. "Then why doesn't Simon swoop in and blast snowballs at the place until they surrender?"

Simon was Beth's consort number two and a dragon. Nice guy. Made the best snow cones.

But he also wasn't a war-mongering, lay-waste-to-the-world kind of fellow. He only went ballistic when Beth was in danger.

He shook his head. "No can do. There are rules about doing that kind of thing." He nicely didn't point out the fact we didn't know where to attack. We only had a vague idea of location.

A week ago, a shaky video of unknown origin surfaced on the internet and appeared to show a massive tank with a bearded merman swimming inside it.

Could be fake. But why then did it get scrubbed from the internet within twenty-four hours? Good thing Jory had a techy friend who'd caught it. He downloaded a copy and kept it on a secure server. Lana spent hours watching it, looking for clues. There were two. One a strange symbol, a lion with a spiked tail and wings on the edge of a computer screen, and two, a coffee cup. The name on it a chain that had stores only in the Rockies.

"Fuck the rules," Lana snapped. "I hate rules."

"I know," placated her mate. "Have a donut." The expression "feed the hungry beast" went triply so for a craving, hormonal siren/mermaid misfit.

While her mouth was full, I jumped in. "Given the restrictions on everyone else, this is why it makes the most sense for me to go. I know those mountains."

"How do you know them?" Beth asked. "I've never seen you travel anywhere."

Because travelling was scary. Another thing my therapist had me working on. "I might have kind of grown up in the Rockies," I admitted.

Lana spat out her donut. Unheard of. "You mean your shithead family lives there?"

"I never said they were shitheads." My mom and dad just didn't understand how their perfect daughter ended up being such a disappointment.

Gone for more than a decade now, I wondered at times how they were doing. I'd only caved twice. I called them not long after I ran, only to tell them I wasn't dead. I hung up before they could talk. The second time was years later before I met my besties and was living on the streets, having a hard time. My mother answered, and I froze. Didn't say a word.

When she whispered "Claire, is that you?" I hung up. I never let myself be that weak again.

Things hadn't changed. I still wasn't a wolf, and my parents deserved better than to have an embarrassment hanging around.

Oh, and a possible killer. But that wasn't the problem of the day.

"You can't confront your family alone," Lana declared.

"Never said I would." Uttered with a roll of my eyes. "No plans for a family reunion." Even if I missed Mother's strawberry rhubarb pie. "However, unlike you and everyone else in this room, I know those mountains." Kind of. I'd grown up in a small town nestled among the peaks. "I can blend in."

For some reason Beth snorted. "You, fit in? You draw attention everywhere you go."

The curse of being adorable—and still very clumsy. But I'd had years to hone my skills in utilizing this aspect to my advantage. "You all need to stop arguing about this. I'm the most sensible solution, especially since we don't even know if this lead is a good one."

That coffee cup could have come from any of five locations. However, Lana wouldn't see reason. She persisted in thinking me incapable. My fault really. I'd recently had stage fright during a demonic kidnapping where the legion of darkness and army of light wanted to kill us.

In my defense, I thought we were goners and saw no point in fighting. However, since that day, I'd made a vow that I would stop being a frightened rabbit. I'd try and be more like good ol' Bugs Bunny, who wasn't afraid of anything.

With that vow in mind, despite being forbidden, and without telling anyone, I packed a bag and snuck out that night. I had to do this, not just for Lana, but myself.

I made it to the hallway, where I found Jory waiting by the elevators, jangling a set of keys. "Lana said to drive you to the airport."

I blinked at him. "She's letting me go?"

"She isn't happy about it and cursed quite a bit. Almost made my ears bleed, but she knows you're the right choice to go scouting."

Pursing my lips, I perused him before declaring, "You tied her to the bed, didn't you?"

His lips quirked. "Maybe."

"She's going to kill you for helping me."

"I can handle it. The question is, can you?" Jory's gaze turned serious, and I appreciated his concern. For a big, war-mongering kind of fellow, he was nice.

"I can do this. I'm not planning on storming a secret base, just locate it. Then I'll call in the cavalry."

"Promise?"

I nodded. I knew my limitations. Floppy ears and

a twitching nose were no match for guns and needles.

"You try and keep Lana calm and in bed. I'll probably only be a few days looking. Week or two at the most." Piece of delicious carrot cake.

CHAPTER 2

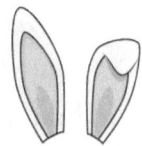

*W*EEKS LATER, *still in the Rockies.*

I wanted to ignore the fact my period was late by a week. Given I was regular as clockwork down to the hour, every four weeks, Tuesday morning, five am-ish, this was unusual and concerning.

I had more important things to do than worry that shark week—a term Lana loved to use and that I'd adopted—decided to not make an appearance. My best friend wasn't the only one to turn feral during that time. I went totally nuts for chocolate, to the point I was ashamed to say I slapped a hand reaching for the M&M's in my bowl. To his credit, Jory didn't slap me back, and Lana just about fell over she laughed so hard.

From then on, as a sort of apology for touching my candy stash, when Jory fetched donuts for Lana, he brought me back a chocolate glazed one, too.

Why couldn't I find a nice guy like that?

Then again, maybe I did find one. What had I done that caused my period to misbehave?

The calendar in the motel room I rented mocked me, the moon fat and round on the Saturday three weeks ago. What had I done that Saturday night by the light of the moon?

I didn't remember. Ever since I'd returned to the Rockies, I'd been randomly shifting and not recalling a moment of it. Kind of concerning. Exactly what kind of stuff was I getting up to when I went floppy eared? And why did it always end in blood?

Not mine, I should add.

The worst part was I'd tried locking myself in my room after the first time it happened, then the time after. After all, a bunny out in the woods was a meal on four feet waiting to be eaten. But somehow, my best-laid plans never worked. I always woke up the following morning, huddled and naked in the woods. Alone with the taste of blood in my mouth.

What did I do? Or should I be asking, who did I do? I almost gagged. Please don't tell me I'd seduced the wildlife. I'd heard horror stories of past examples of this happening. Babies born looking human but with the mind and instincts of an animal.

I peered down at my belly and almost lost my breakfast, which would have been a waste seeing as how it was a delicious chocolate croissant.

Surely there was a logical reason to explain why my period was late. Such as stress. After all, I was on a most important mission. A mission lasting much longer than expected, as each town took a week or more to thoroughly investigate for evidence of a secret medical installation hiding supernaturals.

Why couldn't bad guys post a sign with an arrow stating, "This way to evil secret lab"?

Four towns later and I still had a few more to go because apparently the coffeeshop had expanded, even if their website didn't reflect it. More towns to visit meant I couldn't be pregnant, not only because I had a job to do but because I refused to believe I'd mated with the wildlife and I'd not slept with anyone in months.

So there was no reason to fear the stick I'd peed on.

No reason at all.

No way did I have a baby bunny in my belly.

My nose twitched. The seconds on the clock ticked.

The time was up. I glanced at the little window to see...a star. What the heck? It was supposed to be a line for no, a cross for yes. What was an eight-pointed star?

Defective junk. It probably explained why the pharmacy had the kit discounted along with the several-month-old Easter candies—which, unlike the pregnancy test, still tasted delicious.

I tossed the damned thing in the can and

stretched. Something popped. My stomach cramped, and sure enough, there was my little friend.

The irony wasn't lost on me.

After taking care of business, I buckled down to get to work. AKA, go scouting for information. I had a feeling about this town. And no, it wasn't like the feeling I'd gotten in the last two. Turned out that was too much candy on an empty belly.

Exiting my room, with earphones playing my tune—Rednex, "Cotton Eye Joe," which always made me bouncy—I went for a jog. With no bra.

Slutty, I know, but I did have a reason for it. A few actually. One, I was convinced bras were a tool of evil. I mean, who came up with the idea of putting wires in them and forcing our poor defenseless boobies to be squished and raised all for the visual pleasure of others? Sure, I got great tips when I shoved my girls into a wired contraption, pushing them high enough to rest my chin on. For some reason the men I waitressed for found this worthy of large tips—but nature never intended for our breasts to be imprisoned.

However, that wasn't my main reason for jogging and jiggling my perfect C cups. Today was Friday, and at half past four, happy hour would begin at the pub a few blocks over from my motel. Despite it being late summer, creeping into fall, the patio remained open, mostly so the smokers could gather outside and tar their lungs. Usually, I'd cross the road and avoid that pall of carcinogens hanging in the air, but I was on a mission.

I jogged past and ignored the many whistles. Unlike Lana, I didn't flip the cat callers a bird. Unlike Beth, I didn't suck in all that sexual energy. I kept on going and hit the candy store I'd discovered. They made fresh fudge. Let that sink in.

Fresh. Fudge.

If the owner weren't a happily married woman with grandkids, I'd have proposed. As it was, I had to content myself with buying a huge bag of treats.

I took my time sauntering back, enjoying the fall of twilight as lights came on, giving the world a softer appearance. The sights and smells in this town reminded me an awful lot of the one I grew up in. A bunch of homes built in the sixties and seventies, with brick and vinyl siding to accommodate the factory that supplied the bulk of the jobs, pulp mills being the most common.

Then the save-the-environment folk began to make a stink, and the trade over the border got harder, leading to the demise of those jobs, decimating many towns. I still remembered my dad's face when the mill shut down and everyone was given a pink slip and told to apply for unemployment. But the pack didn't let that setback chase them from the only place they ever knew. Instead, they dipped into their savings and picked up buildings and land for cheap. Including the defunct mill.

When I left, the town was pretty self-sufficient, with most homes retrofitted with solar and wells. The mayor of town, for legal purposes, being my dad. The sheriff, his brother. As to how they earned money? They began new careers in custom furniture and wood carving art.

Weird, right? And yet people would pay big bucks for authentic stuff. And with a thriving trapping trade by the members of the pack who could claim indigenous status, the pack did all right.

This town reminded me of the one I left except it had returned to a bustling era again. Not because of a booming lumber industry. Some kind of research institute was the new bread and butter for this town.

Weird thing, though, Chymera Tech didn't appear on any Google search or map. I didn't even know it existed until I rolled into town and started poking my nose around.

Another interesting fact? None of the locals worked inside the institute itself. Chymera brought in outsiders to man all its medical positions. As to the other jobs such as the guards and cleaning positions? They relied on a temp agency to fulfill the roles and rotated staff every six months.

The town folk didn't seem to mind. The newbies brought their dollars and infused new economic life into local stores, restaurants, and bars.

Bars like the one I had to pass again with my belly full of chocolate and my boobs doing a little bounce. The men were still outside, drinking and smoking. They spotted me right away, but this time when they called me over with whistles and a "Hey, baby, looking fine," I smiled and approached.

"Hi there, fellows, what are you celebrating?"

"It's Friday," exclaimed a corpulent man, raising his bottle of beer in a toast.

"End of the work week?" I teased. "Sounds like a reason to party. Where you guys work?"

"At the medical place in the woods. I'm a scientist," said my new leering friend, only to be jabbed by his buddy.

"Shut it, Larry. NDA," the guy with the comb-over yell-whispered.

Non-disclosure agreement. Sweet. These were just the guys I was looking for, and it looked like Larry probably had the loosest lips of the three. He also had his eyes on my rack, not my face. Predictable.

I worked my flirting magic and soon was sitting with the boys, pretending to drink—because I really didn't have a head for booze—and laughing at their sexist jokes.

Having worked in a bar, I'd heard them all. Especially the blonde ones.

What did the blonde say when she saw Cheerios for the first time? Donut seeds!

Why did the blonde have a hard time dialling 911? She couldn't find the eleven.

What do you call a brunette standing in the middle of a group of blondes? Central intelligence.

Ha. Ha. I pretended to laugh. Some of them were kind of funny. Others just proved why I remained single.

At one point, when I figured my new friend had drunk enough, I leaned in close to Larry and whispered, "Want to go somewhere more private?" Because I had some questions to ask. Questions his annoying friend Johnny—who seriously needed a Tic Tac—and his other bud Fred—who could have used better friends to tell him that the comb-over wasn't working—might object to.

"Yeah. Sure. Now?" Larry's chair tipped over in his excitement to follow me into the dark, quiet alley between the bar and the building next door. The fact he wore a wedding ring didn't slow him one bit. Kind of sad, really, but I couldn't let it stop me.

Larry was my ace in the hole to discovering what happened inside the medical institute since I could find nothing online.

"Where y'all going?" Silly me, I didn't expect his two friends to join us.

I didn't panic. Working in a strip club for years meant I'd learned how to fend off drunken guys who got grabby. Funny how the sight of an owl in a park could freeze me—I hid during the scary parts in *Harry Potter*. But give me a guy who thought I should drop my panties because he said so and I was cool as a frog in a pond.

I turned a faint smile on Johnny and Fred. "Sorry, boys, I wasn't looking for a threesome."

"No worries. I ain't dipping my junk beside Larry's. We'll take turns," said Johnny with a leer.

Ew. That, in my mind, was as bad as sharing a toothbrush, and this was not going according to plan at all. I never intended to actually seduce Larry, just get him to talk. Now that all three of them eyed me with lusty intent, I realized I'd have to abandon my original idea.

"You know what, maybe another time. I have to get up early for work in the morning." I went to move past them, but the men formed a half-circle to ring me in.

"Not so fast, honey. We're not done having fun." Fred no longer looked so drunk, or stupid. His eyes took on a mean cast, bolstered by alcohol. He reached for me.

I slapped his hand. "Excuse me. I don't think so."

It didn't stop them from trying again, and my inner bunny quivered, but I still didn't worry. Past experience proved I might freeze initially when confronted with violence, but I knew at one point I'd snap out of it and save myself.

Before I could go ninja bunny on their asses, a fourth dude appeared. A behemoth to rival Lana's beau.

He might prove to be a problem.

Except he wasn't here to take a turn. "I do believe the lady said she wanted to leave."

"Screw off— Argh." Johnny and his bad breath never finished that sentence since the big dude grabbed and tossed him as if he weighed nothing. Then, with one hand, he shoved Fred with the squinty eyes right into the dumpster. As for Larry with the flat-top hair? He ran. Smart guy.

Except that left only me.

With a guy who'd not yet stated his intentions.

"Thank you," I said, but when I went to move around him, he sidestepped into my path.

Uh-oh. I looked up. Way. Way. Up.

And gasped as I saw his face. "Derek? Is that you?"

CHAPTER 3

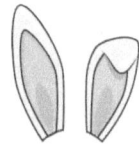

THINKING he'd spotted Claire and actually confronting her were two vastly different things. For one, Derek had been mistakenly seeing her for years now, ever since she ran away from home. As a side note, grabbing a woman by the arm and exclaiming, "Claire, where you been?" didn't go over well with strangers. Luckily, his dad knew the arresting officer, and he'd gotten off with a warning.

But he wasn't hallucinating this time. It really was Claire, in the flesh. She remained just as cute, just as enticing, and just as dumb as before.

Rather than do the nice thing and respond with a "Hey, how you doing?" in a suave voice, he barked, "What the fuck were you thinking, Claire Mahoney? Going into an alley with three drunken asshats? Do you know what might have happened if I'd not come along?"

"Goodness, have you been hitting the juice since

I left? Because someone has rage issues," was her sassy reply.

"I am not taking steroids." However, there was no denying he'd gotten big. Working as a logger for a few years had a way of packing muscle on a guy.

"Then you really should see someone about the anger thing."

"I'm angry because you foolishly did something dangerous. You were about to get raped. Or worse." The very thought caused his rage to continue to boil. A minute later and...

"There's something worse than rape?" she asked.

"Yeah. Getting killed."

"But if I were dead, I wouldn't really care, so can you really say it's worse?"

Did she seriously ask him that? "What are you doing here?"

"What are you doing here?" she countered.

"I live in this town."

"Since when?"

"Since I needed a job. Now, your turn. What are you doing here?"

"I am passing through."

"To where? You going back to see your parents? They've been looking for you." What he didn't say was her parents had grieved hard after she ran. Grieved, searched, and then resolved themselves to losing their child. Thing was, they understood why she'd left.

Everyone did. Claire was different than everyone else. Funny thing was he never cared. He liked her quirkiness. He only wished he'd had a chance to tell her.

"My parents." Her face went through a few expressions: sadness, regret, determination, resignation. "How are they? No." She shook her head. "Doesn't matter. Listen, it was nice running into you." Here came the brush-off. "But I have to go."

"An excellent idea. This town ain't a good place to be sticking around."

"Kind of a shabby endorsement considering you live here."

"Trust me when I say it's not the right kind of place for someone like you."

He knew he'd said the wrong thing the moment she stiffened.

"Like me?" she snapped. "As in, not normal. Weak. Defective."

"That's not what I meant."

"Then what did you mean, Derek?" She planted her hands on her hips and looked about as dangerous as an angry chipmunk.

"I meant not safe for our kind."

"You're staying here," she pointed out.

"Yeah, and in case you hadn't noticed, I'm almost a hundred pounds heavier than you and mean in a fight."

"You don't think I can be mean?" She arched a

brow, and he'd never seen anything sexier. Five foot nothing of cockiness and all woman.

"We both know you wouldn't stand a chance against someone like me."

"You'd be surprised," was her dry reply. "Or don't you remember what happened around the time I left?"

She referenced a past that no one clearly understood. The morning after she left, there was babbling about a creature with great big fangs and a pup missing an ear. Adding to the panic was the fact that no one could locate Claire.

"Is that why you ran?" he asked. "Did the monster in the woods that night scare you?" A monster never seen again, which made many wonder if the pups hadn't just gotten too rambunctious amongst themselves.

"A monster?" she repeated. "Is that what Clive and Jeremy called it?"

"According to them, it was eight feet tall and mean. Slapped them around. Bloodied them pretty good. Clive even lost an ear. Folks thought it got you, too, until you called your parents." The alpha had initially accused Clive and Jeremy of making up the story to cover up the fact Claire was missing and they were involved. Good thing she called to tell them she'd run.

Which was a relief in a sense that she was alive, but in another, a harsh slap to a pack that hadn't realized how their words and actions made her feel. Not her fault she was different. They should have been more accepting. Hell, he should have done more to make her understand. He didn't care if she was cute and cuddly when she shifted. She was also cute and cuddly in human skin too.

A mask dropped down, and her face went blank. "I remember nothing of a monster."

"Then why run away?"

Her lips twisted into a wry smile. "Do you really have to ask that?"

He wanted to say yeah, I gotta ask because you left, and it bummed me out. Being a man in full possession of his balls, he instead mumbled, "You pussied out."

"I would have said hopped while shaking my cotton ball tail, but whatever."

Did she seriously joke? He caught a twinkle in her eyes, and her smile turned genuine. "You should see your face, as if I said a dirty word. And see, that's why I left. You're all serious and feeling sorry for me. But don't you see, I didn't want or need that. I moved on to give us all a chance. Me especially. I made a new life for myself."

"Can't be much of a life seeing as how it's missing your family."

Her lips turned down for a second. "I made new friends that I consider family. Speaking of whom, I'm supposed to be calling Lana in like three minutes, and if I don't, she's liable to send Jory to fetch me."

"Who's Jory?" he grumbled. And why did he have an urge to punch a stranger?

"Big Viking dude. Pretty much married to Lana, although she prefers to call it living in delicious sin. I swear she's gone from prim and uptight to let's not wear panties under a skirt."

He blinked as she babbled.

"Any-hooo, so nice catching up. Looking good by the way. You been working out?" She patted his forearm as she walked past. "Best of luck with your job." She blew him a kiss over her shoulder and sauntered off, a little wiggle in her step. Her butt a heart-shaped thing of cock-hardening perfection.

Tiny and supposedly harmless his ass.

That woman was dangerous.

A good thing she was leaving town.

What was bad for him? The phone call he had to make. Keeping to the shadows, he pulled out his cell and dialed a number he knew by heart.

A familiar voice answered. "Derek? Everything all right?"

Given he'd only called a few times since leaving, he could understand the query. "I saw her."

"Saw who…" A pause then a harsher, "You saw Claire? Where? Is she with you?"

"Not exactly. She's in town. I ran into her by accident on the street."

"How is she? How did she look?" The questions came at him fast and furious from a man who'd lost his daughter and craved nothing more than to see her again.

"She looks good." Better than good. However, that wasn't the kind of thing you said to a woman's father.

"Hold on, you said she's in town. She can't stay there," Garret barked.

Garret was well aware of the missing shifters because Derek kept him informed. Between the two of them, they'd managed to warn and move most of those remaining. But a stubborn few just refused to budge.

"I told her it wasn't safe. She won't leave."

"Won't?" The word seethed through the earpiece. "Make her. She can't stay in the area. She's too delicate to handle what's happening."

Not entirely the word Derek would have used given the bold way she stood up to him, the way she teased. "I'll keep an eye on her."

"Not good enough. We both know you can't watch her twenty-four-seven."

No, he couldn't. He had a job he couldn't quit. "What do you want me to do?"

Silence for a moment. "Did she ask about her mother?" Garret had too much pride to ask for himself.

"It wasn't a long conversation."

"I should fetch her ass and bring it home."

Derek shifted the phone to his other ear. "I don't know if that's a good idea. Let me talk to her. See if I can figure out what's been happening with her."

"I want to know where she's been. What she's been doing."

"I'll do my best to find out. Oh, and check your email. I sent you a picture." Snatched without her knowing, her lips curved in a half smile as she skipped, swinging a bag from a bakery that specialized in sweets.

There was a rustle as his alpha fumbled his phone to check. He heard a sigh. "She's all grown up."

"It's not too late, though," Derek added.

Words that weren't just for his pack leader, but for himself.

Could he have a second chance with the girl he'd fallen for back in high school?

CHAPTER 4

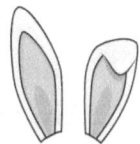

Leaving Derek, I wondered if I'd see him again. Especially since I'd be sticking around.

No way was I leaving town now, not when Derek practically confirmed the fact something hinky was occurring in the area.

Dangerous to shifters. That was what he said, and while his warning might not be related to my quest to find the people holding Lana's parents, it was kind of my duty to find out more. To perhaps raise a warning to my kind so that they weren't placed in danger.

Super altruistic, I know, and super frightening, too. Bunnies weren't supposed to hop to the rescue. We ran. Fast.

The new me, the braver Claire, wasn't about to hide in a burrow waiting for danger to pass. However, making the decision to find out more did not give me immediate answers. I didn't have the slightest clue what Derek meant. Who targeted my kind? Where should I start looking?

In retrospect, I should have asked more questions. Pounced on Derek, pinned him with my body, and tortured the information from him.

With my fingers digging into his flesh.

My lips teasing his.

Teeth nipping.

Um. That sounded more like a recipe for seduction than something that would force him to talk. Beth would totally approve. With her succubus tendencies, she always advised sex for the win.

However, I didn't do casual sex, which might explain why I'd only ever had three real boyfriends and none of them shifters. I went for safe guys. The never aggressive, always passive types who didn't raise their voices even when someone cut them off in traffic.

Boring. I know. Nothing like the excitement of Derek, who oozed menace. Who, with a single dark look, soaked my panties.

Oh no. I was a cliché. Lusting after the classic bad boy. Except Derek wasn't a bad boy, not when I knew him at least. High school jock, yes, but unlike the Clives and Jeremys of the world, he was never mean. To me at least.

He was my first crush, and apparently old feelings didn't die. Seeing him again brought back the same pulse-pounding, fluttery excitement. He was so familiar and yet, at the same time, a stranger.

An impossibility because, despite how he made me feel, my situation hadn't changed. I was still a freak of nature, which meant, no matter how many sparks flew between us, we could never be together.

The keycard to my room turned the light on the handle green, and I entered, only to freeze. A smell lingered in the air. One that wasn't there before. My nose twitched as I tested the air, sifting the different scents, putting aside the ones I knew to focus on, those that did not belong.

Cologne. Something cloying and not mine. Could be the motel staff doing some kind of maintenance. But didn't they usually warn a guest first?

I also caught the faint whiff of cigarette. Gross.

It occurred to me that, in that moment, I couldn't be sure the intruder had left. Perhaps they were still here.

Watching me.

Eek.

My bunny heart fluttered, a rapid beat that threatened to explode from my chest as my gaze darted from side to side. My nose twitched even faster, and my ears were tuned to the slightest sound.

The heating unit for the room kicked in with a banging wheeze, and I squeaked, only barely holding on to my bladder. I'd gotten better about not peeing myself when scared.

I forced myself to take a deep breath. Then another. Reminded myself the odors were faint. Whoever came into my room was probably gone, but just in case, I should check.

Except my feet appeared glued to the floor. I cursed. "Fiddlesticks and cobwebs." Strong words, I know, but they helped snap me out of the fear freezing me. I forced myself to do a circuit.

Nothing pounced on me from the bathroom or closet. No hands grabbed me from under the bed.

The room was empty. I'd scared myself for nothing. Especially since more sniffing revealed whoever had entered my room must have been human— animals, even shifters in human form, had a special smell to them. Whoever entered my space left no unique scent other than the lingering burnt nicotine and cologne.

My stuff appeared untouched, my clothes still spilling out of my bag, my bed perfectly made— because I'd let the maid do her thing earlier that day. It didn't seem as if I'd been robbed. A good thing since I didn't have much to start with. I preferred to travel light.

Never knew when you might have to run in the middle of the night to escape something with a taste for tender bunny flesh.

Paranoia. It was what separated survivors from victims. I couldn't have said if it was my bunny nature or the fact I ran away at a tender age, but I tended to be overly cautious with my safety. Which made the fact I'd even volunteered to come on this mission mind-boggling to those who knew me.

They didn't understand how much I needed to do this.

For all my bouncy and happy outlook, I led a very simple life. Work, home, friends. I carried mace wherever I went. Even on my jogs. I didn't accept rides, candy, or pats on the butt from anyone.

When at work—a strip club that paid above minimum wage with excellent tips—Lana chortled each time my ass got slapped because, for all my fear of everything, I didn't tolerate disrespect. I always handled those inappropriate gestures with a pert and firm, "Please don't touch my posterior or I will have the bouncer toss you out on your head. And yes, I will accept a tip as an apology." I would add that I always delivered the rebuke with a smile and then a thank you as the befuddled man handed over some money.

I should have used my feminine wiles on Derek. Gotten him to spill everything he knew.

Like an idiot, I'd not thought to ask for his address or his phone number. All I knew was he lived somewhere around here.

Which gave me an idea.

It wasn't only wolves who could follow a trail, although usually the prey didn't stalk the predator. Smart bunnies avoided it.

However, he not only gave me a clue about the town having an underbelly, he was the reason I didn't get the information I wanted from Larry. Namely, more details on what happened inside Chymera Tech. Was it a legit lab? Or did they run secret experiments and breeding programs to create impossible hybrids like Beth and Lana?

At least they became misfits on purpose, the doctors had intended to make them different. Me? I had a defective gene to thank. A gene I could pass on to a child and one of the main reasons why I panicked at the thought of being pregnant.

Since I had too much energy to sleep, I quickly changed into more appropriate clothes for skulking—black leggings, slim-fitting black long-sleeve shirt, and a dark cap to cover my blonde hair. Looking delightfully cat burglar-ish, I slipped out of my room. It didn't take long to retrace my steps and find the spot I ran into Derek.

No mistaking the musky aroma of Axe cologne—and man. The very hint of it made me tingle. Probably in excitement at the hunt because I wasn't looking for a boyfriend. And if I were, it would not be a wolf.

The scent he left behind might have been faint, but I managed to follow it—all the while hoping he didn't get in a car and drive away. Lucky for me, he walked.

Across the street, then weaving in and out of

alleys, a strange route, where I encountered no one despite there being plenty of residences. Along the way, I saw the lighted windows of people safe in their homes, the flash of light indicating a television was on. Open windows here and there emitted the murmur of conversation and barks of laughter. I only pulled out my can of mace once when a dumpster rattled. I held it out, ready to spray, only to heave out a breath when a cat poked up its head, rat in its mouth.

The times I hit the sidewalk, I didn't see much traffic or pedestrians. Nighttime was a different beast than the day, especially in this area where there were no bars or restaurants.

It was only as I found herself about to cross the street to the motel that I realized he'd followed me home. A gentleman seeing me home safe, which led to a question.

Is he still trailing me?

I turned to glance behind and saw nothing in the shadows, but I was the first to admit I had terrible night vision.

On a hunch, I planted my hands on my hips and said, "You can come out now. I know you're there."

It took a second more of me wondering if I spoke to thin air before Derek stepped out of the pocket of murk he'd hidden in.

He shook his head, a rebuke if I ever saw one. "I can't believe it took you that long to notice."

Heat burned my cheeks because he was right. I'd not even guessed. Awkward. Which was why I huffed, "I can't believe you stalked me." I was angry, and happy all at the same time. What did it mean that he'd followed me?

He shoved his hands into his pockets and rolled his shoulders. "I wouldn't call it stalking."

I arched a brow.

He grinned. "Okay so maybe it was. I wanted to make sure you got to your place safe."

"And then stuck around."

"Just keeping a friendly eye."

"That was more than a friendly eye, Derek." I might have chastised him, but inside, my tummy was doing Olympic-sized somersaults. What could I say? I thought his actions cute. Chivalry wasn't dead, and it came wrapped in a six-foot-plus delicious package.

"This town ain't safe," he said with a drawl that had super powers. It almost dropped my panties.

"So you said. I want to know what you mean by that. How is it not safe? Does this have to do with the institute?"

"What are you talking about?"

"I think there's something hinky happening at Chymera Tech."

"No idea what you're talking about." His eyes shifted left, and I knew I had him.

"I want to know everything."

"Nothing to tell. And I wouldn't start shit with

them or you'll make folks angry. They bring a lot of business to the area." He began to back away.

"Oh no you don't." I reached out and grabbed him by the arm. A big muscly arm. I might have given it a squeeze. "I'm not done talking to you. Come upstairs with me."

"I don't think that's a good idea." He dug his feet in.

Whereas I held tight to his arm and used all my weight to lean in the direction of the motel.

No surprise, he didn't budge.

"Move," I grunted, holding on to his arm with both hands and heaving.

"I have to go." He pried my fingers loose.

He was going to leave. Suddenly desperate, I bounced into his arms, grabbed his cheeks, and kissed him on the lips.

Wow. Big mistake.

He kissed me back.

Which wasn't the problem.

The fact that I was humming and loving the kiss was. I didn't want to stop. He tasted divine. Felt even better.

He ignited things inside me that whooshed, and I knew he had what I needed to put out that fire.

Still...I wasn't in the habit of kissing guys. Especially not so quickly after meeting them.

Although, technically, I'd known him for years.

Nope. That was a different time. A different me.

We were both adults now. Strangers. And I was still a misfit. He shouldn't get mixed up with me, no matter how good his mouth felt on mine.

Hence why I yanked my mouth free and began walking to my room, a swing to my hips. "You coming?" I purred in my huskiest come-hither voice.

I swear I could feel the heat of his gaze.

"Not fair, Claire," he growled.

"That totally rhymed," I complimented. "You coming upstairs to finish this?" Let him think I meant to continue the kiss. Maybe I would, in the interest of prying more information from his stubborn lips.

"No."

Did he seriously mean that? I cast him a coy glance over my shoulder. It always worked when Beth did it.

He simply glowered at me.

Simmering-hot wolf man. Looking so dangerous. I shivered when he took one step toward me.

Then sighed in disappointment when he turned on his heel and walked in the wrong direction.

So much for getting him to my room to spill his secrets; however, I had won a minor victory.

My kiss, with complimentary grope, had born fruit. I had his wallet. With his driver's license showing an address. Since he wouldn't talk to me, I would simply stalk Derek and see where he went. Who he spoke to. Maybe spot some of the trouble he hinted about.

Smiling to myself, I opened the door to my motel room and walked in.

The cologne smell was back, stronger than before, along with the pungent smoke from a cigarette, but it was the chloroform that worried me most.

"Hel—" The sound was cut off as the cloth was slapped over my mouth.

CHAPTER 5

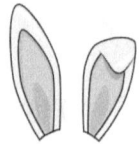

WHY DID I SAY NO? The woman he'd had fantasies about had asked him back to her room, and like a moron, he refused. Strolling away, hands in his pockets, Derek was calling himself all kinds of dumb when he heard it: A faint cry, cut off. Could be anyone, anything. Perhaps a television show. A radio. A complete stranger.

Even before his wolf could raise his hackles, he turned around and jogged back. He emerged from between two buildings to see the taillights of a car and the silhouette of someone leaning over the trunk with something in their arms while another fellow looked on. What did they toss in there?

Probably luggage, and yet something didn't seem right.

Call it instinct. Or just a need to act. His wolf urged speed, and he listened, crossing the road with long strides. He made a beeline toward the car, remaining silent as the two guys opened the car doors. The dome light came on and showed a bald man wearing sunglasses—at night, which caused a certain song to want to play in Derek's head. As for the bald man's companion, he was a brute of a man with a fresh and bleeding scratch on his cheek.

Odd how the mind could home in and focus on details when the adrenaline flowed. How did the man get the scratch? What were they doing here looking so suspicious?

This inquiring wolf wanted to know, so when the car began to move, Derek threw himself in front of it before it could pull out of the parking lot. It braked, the horn honked, and the headlights flashed at him. He held up his hands and shook his head.

The passenger rolled down his window. "Get out of the way, asshole."

"Sure, once you show me what you threw in your trunk."

"None of your fucking business."

"I'm making it my business."

The man with the glasses—the driver—rolled down his window and said, "Nothing suspicious, friend. Just our bags."

Except his gut said it wasn't luggage.

"Prove it. Pop the trunk."

"How about I pop you," threatened the big dude.

"If you've got nothing to hide, then what's the problem?"

"Exactly what do you think we have in there, friend?" The sunglasses fellow remained the calmer voice of reason.

"Looked more like a body than luggage to me."

"Such an imagination. Sorry to disappoint but it wasn't a body."

"Open the trunk." His certainty only grew.

"And if I decline?"

"That's not an option. You aren't leaving until I see what's in there."

Teeth, yellowed by tobacco, gleamed. "And how will you stop me, friend?" Sunglasses gestured to his companion, who emerged from the car, rather taller than expected, wider, too.

He also smelled of a certain lady Derek had recently kissed.

"You really shouldn't have done that," Derek said with a sigh.

"No, he shouldn't have," grumbled Claire before she swung the tire iron at the guy's head. At the first blow the big dude bellowed and began to turn. The second whack had his eyes rolling up, and he fell unconscious on the ground.

Derek just stared as Claire stood over the body, tire iron raised, grinning from ear to ear. A little too maniacally for Derek's comfort. She leaned down and peered through the open door.

"Please, get out," she asked so politely.

Sunglasses pursed his lips.

Derek approached. "You heard the lady. Get your ass out of that car."

"You'll regret this, friend." The guy floored the gas pedal, and Claire squealed as she was knocked away. The car hit the street hard and sped off, the passenger door swinging shut.

He ran to her side. "Claire. Are you hurt?"

"Well, that's a bummer," she lamented. "Why did you let him get away?"

"I'm sorry, I should have stood in front of him and let him run me over."

"That would have been helpful. Where's a tack strip when you need one?" she grumbled. "Next time, while I handle the muscle, you should try and contain the brain."

"Are you seriously giving me shit?"

"There were only two guys. I took care of one, you should have had the other, or was I supposed to do all the work?" She planted her hands on her hips.

He rubbed his face. "You are freaking nuts."

"I'm nuts? That seems harsh given I'm the victim here. Or did you forget I was the one being kidnapped? Good thing I saved myself."

"I was trying to stop them in case you hadn't noticed."

"I noticed you provided distraction by talking a lot." She rolled her eyes.

"How did you get out of the trunk?"

"The emergency latch of course. All the cars have them."

"And does everyone think to grab a tire iron and knock people out with them?"

"Only the smart ones. No need to thank me. I know you're feeling grateful I saved you from what would have been a sound beating."

"Who says he would have beaten me?"

"Did you see the size of his hands?" she exclaimed.

"I've got big hands, too," he snapped, holding them up.

Her gaze dropped. "Big feet, too. Trying to tell me something?"

He gaped. "You did not just say that. That's—"

"Untrue? Are you going to destroy that old wives' tale?"

"Well, no, but still, um," he stammered. Judging by the heat in his cheeks, he blushed.

Whereas she giggled. She also knelt beside the unconscious guy and frowned. "He's going to be heavy to lug around."

"Lug him? Jeezus, Claire, what are you planning to do with him?"

"Question him, of course. We should take him to my room unless you've got a better place. I don't suppose you have access to a torture chamber?"

He gaped.

"Maybe a sex room with restraints?"

Did his bed and some neckties count? "Enough," he barked.

"Enough what? Did I guess right? You *do* have a sex room?" She blinked at him with innocence, but her smile was anything but.

"No. Nor do I have handcuffs or any of that kinky stuff."

"What if you need to tie a woman down?"

"My partners are willing, so no need."

"What if I want to tie you down?" Her lips curved with mischief.

"Again, no need. You want me..." He held out his arms. "Come and get me."

Now it was her turn to look away. She studied the guy on the ground. "We should move him before anyone wonders what's going on. You grab his—"

"Hey, you need help out there?"

A nosy motel neighbor poked his head from his room. His white tank top pristine, his hair on end, and his yellow boxers sporting a happy face.

"No worries. I think he had too much to drink," Claire hollered.

"We were just going to take him to his room," Derek added.

The nosy guy came out of his room and leaned over the body. "I think he needs more than his bed. That's a nasty bruise on his head he got from falling. Betty!" he bellowed. "Call an ambulance."

There was no dissuading Happy Shorts. An

ambulance was called, the guy taken away on a stretcher, and since they weren't related, neither of them could go with the medics or even find out his name.

Within twenty minutes, the guy was packed off in an ambulance, leaving Derek to see Claire to the door of her room.

"Sorry we lost him. Maybe we can go see him at the hospital later and see if he'll talk."

She snorted. "As if his partner in crime won't spring him out of there within the hour."

Valid point. "Why were they kidnapping you?"

"Because I'm awesome." A boast he didn't disagree with.

"Seriously, Claire. Did they say anything to you?"

"Nope. They just slapped some chloroform on my face, and I was out like a light."

"You recovered pretty quick."

"Yeah, I metabolize stuff quickly on account of my bunny genes."

"I'm glad you weren't hurt," he said.

"Me, too." She smiled and, for a moment, looked just like the sweet girl he used to know. A girl who didn't go around whacking guys with tire irons.

"Took a lot of guts to protect yourself like that." He delayed his departure, not ready to leave her quite yet.

"More than you know. I have a problem with freezing sometimes when I get scared."

"Well, you didn't freeze tonight."

"No, I didn't. And I didn't turn into a cotton ball ninja."

He snickered. "I can just imagine the terror on their faces had you gone floppy-eared and hopped away."

"You have no idea." Said in a dry tone.

"So, did you want me to come inside, maybe check the place over, make sure no kidnappers stayed behind?" No use denying it. He didn't want to leave. Heck, he should have never refused her earlier invitation.

Her nose twitched once, and she licked her lips, indecision on her face. She shook her head. "I'm good. There's no one else here."

"You should let me stay. What if they come back?"

"I know how to protect myself. Bye, Derek. Nice seeing you again."

Bye?

She meant it. The door shut in his face, and he stared at it long enough to seem creepy-stalkerish before he turned away. He debated parking his ass across the street. Since the kidnapping had failed, he doubted they'd try again that same night. But what about tomorrow?

He needed to convince Claire to leave town.

The sooner, the better because, apparently, she was on someone's radar.

Which meant they'd try again, and next time, he might not be around to see her kick some ass.

Seriously. Little Claire with the bright smile had taken down that guy as if it were nothing.

He didn't know if that turned him on or frightened the hell out of him.

Problem was, now that he'd seen her again? He couldn't stop thinking about her. Once upon a time, he'd lusted after a pretty girl. Now he lusted after the woman.

Once he reached home, he discovered nothing could distract him from thoughts of her. His cock especially refused to quiet down. Semi-erect and annoyed he'd not done more to pursue that fine ass.

Only one thing to do since he couldn't have Claire. His pants hit the floor, and he wrapped his hand around the hard length of his cock. He stroked the velvet skin, hand sliding up and down, picturing instead her smaller fingers on it. Perhaps those perfect lips poised for a kiss.

The very thought brought a pearl of liquid, which he spread over the head of his shaft. A shaft that would have loved to have her tongue lapping at it.

He closed his eyes and could picture it so easily. Claire on her knees, fingers gripping his dick, her mouth open wide, ready to take his rigid length deep. The heat of her as she sucked.

She still had that amazing golden hair. Hair he wanted to grab. Feel. He'd wager it was soft as silk.

Every part of her would be silken and sweet. Would she cry out if he lapped at her cunt? Would she grab at him and urge him to take her?

To fuck her.

Derek groaned and stroked his cock faster, a tight fist around it, pumping up and down with almost manic speed.

He had to wonder if she would swallow when he came, or would she present her luscious tits to him, a landing spot for his cream?

Or would she want him to thrust into her? Drive his cock into that sweet pussy of hers, fingers digging into his back, her hips and body undulating under him until she screamed his name.

He came. Hard. And barely managed to catch his cum with his T-shirt. But his cock didn't wilt. It remained semi-hard. His mind still full of Claire.

Beautiful. Curvy. Claire.

He knew in that moment he had to see her again.

CHAPTER 6

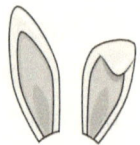

I slept like a baby—after I secured the motel room; wedging a chair under the doorknob. Since I couldn't do the same to the bathroom window, I scattered toiletries on the bathroom floor. Tripping hazards that would make some noise if someone tried to climb in. I took notes during Home Alone and expanded upon that boy's brilliance.

As to the window at the front, it was sealed shut with silicone. The only way someone would get in was by smashing it. The breaking tinkle of glass should wake me if someone were that brazen.

Only once I felt safe did I crawl into bed.

All that adrenaline I'd used fighting off the drug and then combatting my terror needed replenishing. My head hit the pillow, and I fell into a deep sleep.

One filled with dreams. All featuring Derek.

No surprise. A chance meeting, a stroll down memory lane, and then a scorching kiss? Add in the fact he wanted to come to my rescue, and when I woke, was it any wonder my hand crept under the covers?

Bad hand. I was not going to masturbate to the thought of Derek. I'd had my chance to invite him in for the real thing, but I decided to act responsibly instead.

A shower was the thing I needed to clear my mind and cool off. However, the lukewarm shower did nothing for my raging libido. I couldn't stop thinking of the kiss.

That electric kiss. And the feel of him, so big and strong. The fact he was a wolf only added to my excitement. He was dangerous.

Sexy.

A distraction.

Oh heck. There was no point fighting it. I apparently wouldn't be able to think straight until I took care of business. I leaned against the cool tile and closed my eyes. All the better to picture Derek.

I ran my hands over my body, and the weird thing was, no matter how many times I touched myself, I enjoyed the exploration. The sensation of my fingers gliding over slick wet skin.

I cupped my breasts, a nice handful, not entirely firm. I squeezed them and totally pretended it was Derek's callused hands fondling me. A brush of my thumb over the nipples and they hardened. A jolt hit me between the legs at the thought of him sucking the tips. Drawing those pointed peaks into his mouth.

A hand slid down my body as I imagined him working my nipples with his teeth and lips. Bet he was a biter.

My hand slipped between my thighs, and it wasn't just the water making me slick. My fingertip ran over my sensitive nub, and my breathing quickened. I rubbed, feeling my flesh engorging, my pussy clenching. My other hand slid between my thighs, and I penetrated myself with two fingers.

Thrust in and out as my finger worked my clit. Wishing Derek was here on his knees sucking at my sex. Or even better, pumping his shaft into me.

He was big and strong enough to lift me and bounce me on his cock. He'd stroke me deep and hard.

My fingers worked faster, and my whole body quivered with arousal. My pussy was slick with cream, but my orgasm hung just out of reach.

Angling my hips let me push deeper, and I gasped.

But it wasn't enough. I needed more.

I fantasized about what Derek would do next. Tossing me onto a bed, pulling my legs up to rest on his shoulders, exposing me to him.

Oh.

He'd slam his cock into me. Deep. Hard. He'd

pump me, grinding against my sex, hitting me in that sweet spot. Over and over and...

I came, the force of the flex squeezing my fingers. My knees trembled, and I sank to the floor of the shower, my body riding the ebbing wave of my orgasm.

An orgasm that left me dissatisfied. Probably because it wasn't the real thing.

And it would never be the real thing because I couldn't get involved with Derek. He remembered me as sweet Claire Mahoney. He had no idea of the things I'd done. What I was capable of doing.

I couldn't bear to see the look on his face if he did.

Frustrated and with too much energy to burn, I threw on my jogging gear.

Chocolate and candy wasn't the only thing I loved. Running came a close second.

Nothing like getting the blood flowing and my muscles tingling with a good jog, especially on a fresh and dewy morning. The sight of frost on the ground wasn't daunting. Crisp air filled my lungs. My legs pumped, along with my arms. I followed a path I'd mapped out.

It took me right by Derek's house. According to his driver's license, he lived at 452 Eighteenth Street. As I ran past, I took note of the single-story home. No garage, just a driveway with a pickup truck. No flowers or bushes in the front. Just a lonely pine tree. Someone needed a landscaper in a bad way.

The front window had the vertical blinds closed. I saw no light, but it was bright enough outside to not need any lamps.

Since standing and staring might freak out the neighbors—and cops never did like the excuse I was admiring the roof tile—I kept going. Feet hitting the pavement with a steady thump. The music in my ear buds helping me keep a pace.

My entire body hummed, and my mind spun. What would I do today? I'd yet to get any good leads, but my gut told me I was in the right place. And no, this had nothing to do with Derek.

Okay, so maybe it did, but only because I truly believed he might know something. He warned me I should leave and look what happened. Someone tried to kidnap me! Which I hadn't told Lana about yet. She'd have ordered me home and not taken no for an answer.

However, the fact that someone tried to abduct me only convinced me I was on the right track. Which was why I'd be visiting the hospital later to find out more about the big dude who jumped me the previous night. I'd better bring some bakery treats for a bribe because hospitals were weird about not giving out info, citing privacy and stuff. Good thing I knew how to talk and smile my way into getting the basics. All I needed was a name.

On my return trip back past Derek's house, I found him standing at the end of his driveway, newspaper tucked under an arm. Coffee cup in hand.

As I slowed in front of his place, he held out the mug.

"Is that for me?" I glanced at the very light-colored brew.

"Triple sugar with cream."

"How did you know?"

"Wild guess based on your treat bag from last night."

"Awesome." I took a sip. Mmm. Real sugar, none of that fake no-calorie no-carb stuff. "But how did you know I'd be jogging this way?"

"Because you're not exactly subtle when you spy. Since my neighbors don't like people who skulk, I thought I'd invite you in for breakfast."

"I do not skulk! Just out for a morning run."

"Here?" He gestured to the street lined with houses. "There's a park with trails one block from the motel."

"Boring," I sang.

"River about six blocks the other way."

"Seen one river, seen them all."

"Why not just admit you wanted to see me again?" He winked. "It's okay. I totally get it. I can't stop thinking about the kiss either."

"Yeah, but did you masturbate to it?" I sassed. His plan to throw me off guard backfired.

He gaped. His cheeks got color, and I gasped. "Oh my, you jerked one off, didn't you? Don't feel bad. I let my fingers do some walking, too, if you know what I mean." I winked.

"You are impossible. Get inside," he grumbled before giving me a tap on the butt with his paper.

"Eep," I squeaked even if it didn't hurt. "You should not be doing that. I didn't give permission."

"Get inside or I'll do it again."

"Don't you dare."

"I will dare if you don't move."

He seemed serious, which was cute, and while I was tempted to stay still for another little pat on my butt, I wouldn't mind breakfast. My cash flow was running low, which meant I needed to find some work to get flush again. I could call Lana and she'd wire me some, but then I'd get the whole speech about how I should give up and come home. That was the last thing I wanted to do.

Lana did not need a third wheel cramping her time with Jory. She'd finally found the guy who made her sing happy songs that brought the birds and didn't kill them.

Plus, it was time I went out and had my own adventure and me time. I'd spent the last few years kind of stuck in a rut. Not going outside my comfort zones.

Seeing first Beth, then Lana, being dragged out and forced to act and, in the process, finding love, made me realize I'd never find my sweet spot in life if I didn't do something.

If it took going across the Rockies, town by town, looking for something to make my restless feet slow down, then so be it.

I was having fun.

As for the dangerous part, like almost being kidnapped? Kind of exhilarating.

Running into Derek?

Panty wetting.

Seeing him again in a tracksuit that did nothing to hide his body?

Delicious.

The offer of food?

I strutted into his house like I owned it. Only to stop dead. Because what did I see on the table in his kitchen? Two bowls and a box of bran flakes.

I turned a horrified face toward him. "You cannot seriously expect me to eat that."

"It's healthy," he countered.

"It's fiber," I gasped, as he didn't seem to understand the gravity of it.

"Yes, and?"

"Where are the Froot Loops? The Captain Crunch? Or Honeycombs? And bacon. It's not breakfast if there's no bacon dipped in syrup."

"Sugar and fat?" His turn to appear horrified.

"Oh, dear me. Don't tell me you're one of those who bought into the whole hype about sugar being bad. It should have its own food group. We need to fix this, pronto. Please tell me you have flour, baking soda, eggs, and milk."

"I don't bake, so no flour, but I do have eggs and milk."

"Nutmeg and cinnamon?" I pled.

"I've got some kind of spice mix for spiked eggnog if that helps."

It did. Especially since I'd spotted a loaf of bread on the counter. In moments, I'd whipped up some fluffy French toast, heated some jam to syrup consistency, and plated it along with tall glasses of milk.

He eyed the half-dozen slices on his plate. I only had four, my concession to the fact he was bigger.

"That's a lot of food," he remarked.

"Eat." I didn't hesitate any longer, digging in and humming my way through the plate and then scraping the leftover jam from the bottom with my fork. I looked over to see him only a third of the way through his stack.

"You don't like?" I asked.

"It's good, but I'm not that hungry." He gestured.

I took it as an invitation and grabbed two more off his plate. Then when he had only a few more bites before putting his fork down, I slid the remainder my way and dug in as well.

"How do you do it?" he finally asked.

"Do what?"

"Eat all that and stay—"

"Don't say skinny. I hate that word."

"You're not fat."

"Nope. I like to think of myself as just right. I have a very high-acting metabolism." I finished off the last bite and then, because I couldn't resist, swiped my finger over the jam on the plate and licked it.

I noticed him watching the movement of my finger. So for fun, I licked it again.

He swallowed, and his expression turned lusty.

How sexy.

And totally counter to my promise to not sleep with him. I blamed him for that. He just had to make himself irresistible. Which was mean. I had addiction issues when it came to yummy things.

"Well, that was delicious," I declared. "But we'll have to go shopping before lunch."

"Lunch?"

"You invited me in. I assumed you had a morning of things planned."

"No. I've actually got to get to work." He rose from his chair. "As it is, I'm gonna have to speed or I'm going to be late. But you can hang out here if you'd like. I guess."

"That would be weird. I mean, what if your girlfriend popped in to surprise you and found me?" Last night when I kissed him, I'd not wondered if he had someone else.

Now, it was imperative for me to know.

"I'm single. No roommate. So feel free to hang here. Make yourself at home."

I cocked my head. "You're worried those kidnappers will be back."

"You should be, too. I called the hospital. They already discharged the guy you clocked."

"I can handle myself."

"They might be better prepared next time."

"Then you'd better check on me when you're done working to make sure I'm safe. You know my room number. Chinese food might make your overbearingness endurable."

"Is that a hint to bring you dinner?"

"Was it too subtle? Because I will be expecting some. With fortune cookies. And lots of sweet and sour sauce for the eggrolls."

"I'll bring you food if you promise to go back to the motel and stay inside. Don't let anyone in. It's not safe."

"So you keep saying and yet I've not heard why."

"I'll tell you when I see you tonight."

"Why not tell me now?"

He smiled at me, a slow, sexy thing that made my girly bits tingle. "Because this way you'll be thinking of me all day long."

The joke was on him. I was going to think of him anyhow.

He offered to drive me back to the motel, but I knew

he was running late for work, and besides, now he would be thinking about *me* all day long. Wondering if I was safe. Maybe I'd text him a picture of me in the shower...

Because I did manage to score his phone number, right after I returned his wallet—so he could buy me dinner later.

With my belly full, I wandered around for a while. My motel room only had a television. As if I wanted to lie in bed and watch it all day. I'd rather explore. So I did, walking in and out of shops. Talking to people. Learning that Chymera Tech had only been around for about five years, so not the place Lana was once held in. But that meant nothing. Businesses changed locations all the time.

At the grocery store, I discovered someone had been picking up large shipments of groceries. As in a thousand dollars' worth of stuff every few days. But the guy wouldn't say what or who it was for.

Apparently, the big grocery client was due back tomorrow for another load. I made a mental note to return. Maybe with Derek since he had a vehicle we could use to follow.

Me, I wasn't allowed a license on account I just couldn't handle driving and existing at the same time. The world should really thank me for deciding to remain a passenger.

Eventually, as the afternoon waned, I walked back to the motel and waved to Mr. Happy Underpants and his wife as they exited their room and got in their car.

I bounced up the stairs to my room, slid my keycard in the door, and then paused before going inside.

With Derek coming over, it might be smart to invest in some protection, just in case things got frisky. Lucky me, there was a vending machine in the motel office that offered three sizes. I was heading back down the stairs when an explosion overhead sent me flying.

CHAPTER 7

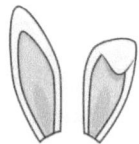

THE DAY JOB DRAGGED. Acting as a guard for the forty or so staff and rare guests at his work didn't make for a busy time.

More than once Derek's mind strayed to Claire.

Sweet Claire who put away a stack of French toast with an enjoyment that shouldn't be seen outside the bedroom. Made a man wonder what sounds she'd make when he licked her top to bottom and buried his face between her thighs.

He still couldn't believe she'd brazenly stalked his house. How about the fact she'd stolen his wallet the night before? He'd not even noticed until she handed it over before walking out his door.

How many skills had she acquired since she'd left their hometown? Because this Claire, this bubbly, ultra-confident woman, while the same sweet girl he'd once admired from afar, had hidden depths.

Work ended at five o'clock, with the evening guy taking over. On the way into town, Derek stopped and snared Chinese food, getting three times what he'd usually get himself. Best to be safe. He also stopped at the store and picked up the sugariest-looking cereals he could find, along with a box of cookies. Something chocolate covered with marshmallow and jam inside.

Armed with treats, he headed to the motel, a country station crooning on the radio, his hand beating the steering wheel in time. As he turned onto the street she was staying on, he slowed in shock. Where once had sat a bright blue two-story monstrosity, there was now a single story because the top floor was a smoldering ruin.

Firemen wearing their suspenders, jackets open to show shirts stained in soot, coiled a hose back onto a truck. A police car sat in the lot, lights slowly flashing as the officers stretched caution tape from light pole to hydrant to another pole, blocking the area in the hopes of barring people from approaching the wreck. As if that would stop the curious. They crowded the sidewalk and held out their phones, taping the scene, their excited chatter filling the air. Some stood by suitcases, evicted patrons. He scanned the crowd looking for one particular face but didn't spot it.

Where was Claire? Panic, a rare emotion for him, fluttered inside, along with cold fear.

I never should have left her alone.

He hopped out of his truck and sauntered right up to the plastic yellow caution line. "Excuse me?" Derek called out to the officers. "What happened?"

"Fire." Said in a duh, kind of obvious tone.

"Were there any casualties?" Then because the cops were eyeballing him, he hastened to add, "A friend from out of town was staying here. A woman. Blonde. About yay high." He held up his hand about pec high.

The rude cop shrugged, but the officer with the dark skin took pity on him and replied, "Everyone got out in time far as we know."

"Were they sent somewhere?"

"Yeah," the first cop said, suspicion in his gaze. "And before you ask, we won't be telling you where. Privacy and all. I'm sure your friend will call you."

Would she? His phone hadn't rung all day. Which meant nothing. She might have chosen not to call. Or she could be burnt to a crisp.

The idea didn't sit well, and he tried to focus on what the officer had stated, which was no one got trapped inside. But where did she go if she escaped?

Sticking around would probably only get him hauled in for questioning, so he sped off. With no clue where to begin looking for Claire, he went home. Let himself in and paused at the knife hovering chest high in front of him.

The smile behind it didn't reassure.

"What the fuck, Claire?"

"Hey, Derek. About time you got home. And you brought food. I might just love you," she squealed as she dove on the bags, the knife waving around in a dangerous fashion.

Meanwhile he froze at the word love. He knew she didn't mean it. Yet it evoked the strangest feeling.

"Why do you have a knife?" Had someone attacked her?

"I was getting ready to cut up some fresh brownies I made."

Which, now that she mentioned it, filled the air with a baking decadence he'd not enjoyed since leaving home.

"What happened at the motel?" he asked.

"Someone blew up my room," she announced, heading off with the bags.

"Hold on a second. What do you mean someone blew up *your* room? How did you escape?"

"The bomb was on some kind of delay. My keycard triggered it. Except I didn't go inside on account I forgot something. And then boom!" She exploded her hands. "Whole thing blew up. The impact sent me flying. Good thing I know how to hit the ground. Best thing I ever learned as a kid."

"Your dad taught you to tumble?"

She snorted as she tore apart the paper bags. "As if. I was daddy's princess. He never did anything with me that might get me dirty. It was my mom who taught me. Some of the time her tricks work."

"What do you mean some of the time?"

She slid plates onto the table before replying. "The bunny in me isn't a brave creature. Its first instinct is to freeze, and if that won't work, then it tends to want to hide. Doing anything other than that goes contrary to my nature."

"You didn't look frozen or afraid when you took out that guy."

"I've been working on the whole statue and flight bit."

"Working on being badass?"

She smiled. "You might say that. Since my therapist is back home, I've been listening to some self-help tapes while I sleep. Which I guess got blown up. Pity. I was just about to start the section on not panicking in crowds. Oooh, lemon chicken." As the yummy food came into view she was distracted.

The lack of conversation while they chewed gave him time to digest, and he didn't mean the food. Someone had tried to kill Claire, and she didn't seem bothered by it at all.

It bothered the hell out of him, though.

For the next little bit, talk revolved around her delight in the food. He'd chosen well. The lemon chicken tempura breaded with a sweet lemon sauce, the chicken balls crispy with a cherry sauce for dipping. Then there was the honey beef. And the garlic ribs. She dove into all of it, even the vegetables. She took special delight in rolling her eggroll in the plum sauce and then sucking it off before biting.

The woman made eating into a spectator sport.

"Aren't you hungry?" she asked, pointing to his plate. He'd only had one serving.

"I'm fine. You?" Because they were running out of food.

"Perfect. For now." She leaned back and patted her belly. "Don't forget, I made brownies for later."

"Later." It occurred to him that, while she had chosen to come to his place after the explosion, she'd not told him how she got in, or what she planned next.

"How did you get in? Don't tell me lock picking is another hidden talent."

"Don't be silly," she snickered. "I took your spare key last time I was here."

What? He glanced at his pegboard, and sure enough, the spare was gone. "You took my key." He shook his head. "I'm beginning to think you have klepto tendencies."

"Me? I never steal. But I do borrow from friends."

Friends. Hunh. The very idea gave him another warm feeling, but he had to wonder if theirs could be the kind of friendship that came with benefits.

"You staying the night?" he asked.

"I'd say that was obvious."

What was less obvious was where she'd sleep. He had no couch, opting for a pair of leather chairs. He'd tackle that problem later.

"I guess with your stuff all burnt to a crisp, you'll have to go back home. Where is home, by the way?" She'd not yet said.

"Home is an apartment hundreds of miles away. And I'm not ready to go back there yet. Not to mention, I can't leave until I can clear this town."

"Clear it of what?" he asked.

She leaned forward on the table, her expression earnest. "Can you keep a secret? A really big one."

Stupid question. He eyed her askance. "Do you really have to ask that? You know I'm a werewolf, right?"

"That secret is one thing. I'm about to tell you something huge. Something people aren't aware of and would freak about if they knew."

"Are you about to tell me aliens exist?"

She snorted. "Everyone already knows that."

"I was joking."

"I'm not."

He stared at her. "Aliens aren't real, Claire."

"Neither are giant bunnies and werewolves." She winked. " Now are you going to promise?"

"Would you like me to pinky swear?" He held up his little finger.

She hooked hers around it. "Swear you won't tell

anyone. Because I promised Lana I'd keep this on the down low."

"Lana being?"

"My roommate. The one I'm doing this favor for. I promised her I'd only gather intel."

"Intel on what?" he asked, getting exasperated.

She tugged his little finger. "Swear first.

"Fine. I swear I won't tell anyone anything you tell me. No matter how crazy it sounds."

"Are you calling me crazy?"

"As a rabbit."

Her lips twitched. "Good enough. So get ready." She took in a deep breath. "There's a group of humans, scientists and doctors and maybe even the military, kidnapping supernaturals, shifters, and other peeps, and conducting experiments with them. Even breeding impossible species for an unknown purpose."

"Shit. Are you sure about this?" He'd known about the missing shifters, but to hear the reason why... It took him by surprise. It also made him even more worried about Claire.

"Yes." She nodded. "Very sure. Which is why I'm here. I think that Chymera Tech is one of their secret hideouts."

"What makes you think that?"

"It's a medical institute," she stated.

"And?"

"They do medical things."

"Doesn't make them a front for evil scientist plots," Derek pointed out.

"You don't believe me," she grumbled.

"Oh, I believe you. After all, I did warn you there was shit happening in this town. But the institute is legitimate."

"How would you know?"

"Because I work for them."

CHAPTER 8

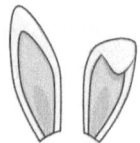

I OGLED THE MAN, not just because his ass looked mighty fine in his black khakis with tons of pockets—which would come in handy for stashing candy if we went to the theater and wanted to avoid overpriced candy—but because one, he didn't even blink when I said people were being kidnapped for evil experiments. And two...

"You mean this entire time you've been working for Chymera and didn't tell me?"

"You seem to forget we only ran into each other twenty-four hours ago. Plus, you never asked."

"I asked what you were doing here."

"I told you. Working."

"You didn't say you were working for a devious conglomerate intent on harvesting our genes for unknown purposes."

"We don't know they're harvesting genes, but I'd say their purpose is the usual one. Wealth."

"Well, now that I know you have an in, what are we waiting for? Take me to the bad guys' headquarters."

"Back up a second, Enny."

"Enny?" I wrinkled my nose. "My middle name is Beatrice. Where did you get Enny from?"

"Short for Energizer because, damn, you talk and move a mile a minute. Slow down for a second."

"Why slow down? Slowing down doesn't get stuff done. I'm a believer in multi-tasking, which is why I brush my teeth in the shower."

"Because brushing your teeth is such a time waster. Why not pee while you're in there, too?" His remark oozed sarcasm.

My smile was slow and mischievous as I said, "Who says I don't?"

Totally worth his dropped jaw. Which I lifted for him before patting him on the cheek. "Try and keep up. That is if you can. Do wolves have some version of Scooby snacks to give them a lift?"

"I don't need a cookie. What I want to do is not go off half-cocked. We have to be careful. Have you forgotten someone tried to kidnap you and, when that didn't work, attempted to kill you?"

"Could be totally unrelated."

"They're related."

"If that is the case, then we need to move while we have the element of surprise. Right now, whoever placed that bomb trying to silence me so I won't go to the cops is probably assuming I died in that fire. Now is the perfect time to infiltrate and catch them off guard."

"Infiltrate what? I told you the place is legit. They aren't hiding shit. Hell, they give tours once a month."

"What if it's a front?"

"Now you're stretching."

"I say it's the right place. It's the perfect cover. They've got the equipment, the people. There's probably like a dozen subbasement levels where they hide their experiments."

He stared at me. "There is no basement."

"That you know of, because it's hidden, silly. But I must be on the right track. Why else try to kidnap me? They probably wanted to use me in their breeding experiments." Joke was on them though. My DNA was defective.

"If they wanted shifters, then why go after you and not me?" he asked. "After all, I've been here longer."

"Maybe they don't need guys."

"Or could be the kidnapping thing has to do with something else."

"You think those guys wanted to sell me to some sheik for his harem? It wouldn't be the first time. Good thing I have an embedded GPS. Lana came to rescue me before the container was put on the boat. Those poor sailors, though." I shook my head. The doctors never did have a theory on how all their eardrums burst at once."

"You've been kidnapped before?"

"Twice. The second time was by a demon using me as bait to draw Beth to Limbo."

"A demon?" Repeated with a hint of skepticism.

"Yes, a demon in cahoots with an angel. They wanted to prevent Beth from becoming Queen of Limbo, which she renamed Misfitia, on account, like me, she never felt like she fit in." All true, but his poor incredulous expression told me he didn't believe a word. Understandable. Until recently, I didn't know demons existed either. Ugly fellows who could really use some external exfoliation and mouthwash. "Anyhow, I was just pointing out the validity of your point that my kidnapping could be for all kinds of reasons, except for one thing."

"And that would be?"

"This." I pulled out a key card—pure black with just a little golden symbol in the corner—that despite being smudged reminded me an awful lot of the one I'd seen in the video that sent me here.

"Where did you get that?" he barked, snatching it from me.

"Filched it from the big dude's pocket before the EMTs took him away."

"That's an access card."

"Duh. I'll bet it gets us into whatever secret building they're doing their experiments in."

"Again, making assumptions. It could be for anything. Even a hotel room."

I shook my head. "Come on, even you've got to admit the evidence is stacking up."

His lips flattened. "Let's say you do find the place that card belongs to. If it is some sort of secret lab, then it will have guards."

"Hence where you can help. You can be the muscle."

"And apparently the brains since this is nuts. You can't just go around looking for the people who kidnapped you."

"If I don't, who will?"

"Anyone but you." He shook his head. "We should tell those in charge." By in charge he meant my dad, and above my dad, the werewolf king. Who was currently a queen on account she killed her husband for cheating on her with a younger bitch.

"Those in charge have known about this and done nothing for decades. What happened to Lana and Beth happened ages ago."

"Perhaps they didn't know."

"And people call me naïve." I sniffed.

"If what you're saying is true, then you are talking about a complex group who's been able to successfully hide for a long time. You can't just expect to waltz in and dismantle them."

"Never said I was planning to. I told you, I'm after intel."

"And what will you do with that intel?"

"Call in people who can handle it."

"Who are these people?"

Rather than reply, I hit the freezer for the tub of cookie dough ice cream I'd stashed in it earlier. Right beside the Creamsicles and Fudgsicles.

"Want some?" I showed the tub to him.

He shook his head.

His loss.

A dollop on a brownie I warmed in the microwave meant sweet goodness in my mouth.

He stared at me as I ate, and just in case he thought of stealing a bite, I curled my arm around my dessert bowl.

"You didn't answer my question. Who are you calling if you find something?" he asked tersely. Probably on account he regretted not getting his own bowl of orgasm for the tongue.

"Let's just say I know people. Tough people." I left it vague rather than mention the fact that a horde of Vikings was likely to stampede into town ready to take out the bad guys.

I spooned more of my dessert into my mouth and noticed him staring again. Watching my lips, his eyes getting a hot glow to them.

In turn, it ignited something inside me, a warm spot between my legs that tingled.

He reached forward, and his thumb brushed my

lower lip. "You have a spot of chocolate." He licked it.

I melted a bit more. "Did you..." My voice emerged husky. "Did you get it all?"

His lips curved into a slow smile. "I think I missed a spot."

He leaned in closer this time, brought his mouth right up to mine, and kissed me.

Kissed me with a languorous passion that had me sighing and angling forward. I wanted to get closer. I reached for him, my hand curling around his neck, my body craned over the table, my boob rubbing against melting ice cream.

The cold shock had me pulling away.

I looked down at my shirt. The wet ice-cream spot glaring.

Leaving me with a choice. I could walk away, right now. The right thing to do. Or...

I pointed. "You missed another spot."

A groan rolled out of him as he hit the floor on his knees, still tall enough that he could pull me forward and latch his mouth to the damp, sugared fabric. He sucked, not just the shirt but my breast, tugging at the erect nipple. Drawing it deep while I gasped. My fingers threaded his hair as he suckled, and then I gasped again as he switched to the other side.

His actions ignited my libido. I burned. Wanted.

I might have made a pleading sound. He

pushed back enough so he could bring his face lower. His big hands parted my thighs, and he put his head between them. I still wore pants, and yet that didn't stop him from putting his mouth on me. I felt it.

Shuddered at the sensation. Shuddered again when he blew hotly, pushing that warm air past my pants and panties right to my pussy.

He sucked at my cleft. Massaging it with his mouth, teasing me.

"Derek." I panted his name. Wanting more. Wanting him.

He drew me from the chair into his lap. He had me sitting with my back to him, my head leaning on his shoulder, exposing my neck to his lips. As for his hands... They roamed. One hand cupping and kneading my heavy breast, rolling the nipple and pinching. His other hand slid past the waistband of my pants, past the skimpy edge of my panties, and through my tuft of curls.

When his finger found my clit, I cried out, and his lips sucked harder at my skin.

I undulated as he fingered me, his rough digit alternating between my engorged nub and dipping into my pussy itself.

My pleasure built as he played with me. The hardness of his erection pushed at my buttocks, and yet he didn't seem worried or in a rush. He kept stroking me. Sucking me. Penetrating me. His fingers pumping in and out until I came with a cry that sounded an awful lot like his name.

And still he teased, keeping that orgasm rolling as he whispered in my ear, "Think you can handle the big bad wolf?"

Could I ever!

Before I could see if he was as well-endowed as he felt, my phone rang. The ringtone—a rousing rendition of "Under the Sea"— let me know it wasn't a call I could ignore. Because if I did, Lana was liable to send a Viking army into the Rockies looking for me.

"I'm sorry. I have to take this." I rolled out of his lap and didn't dare look at him. Couldn't with my pussy still throbbing, which might be why I was more terse than usual when I answered, "Shark Buffet, all you can eat mermaid sushi on the menu today."

"Your motel blew up!" were the first words I heard bellowed.

"Yeah, I—"

"How come you didn't call? Do you have any idea how worried I was when I saw that report?"

"Sorry I—"

Lana wasn't listening to anything I had to say, and I didn't really care because I was more interested in the soft kiss dropped on my nape and Derek's whispered, "That was the best dessert I've ever had."

I almost tossed the phone and demanded

seconds; however, if I did, Lana would lose her ever-loving mind. Derek left the kitchen, and a second later, I heard the shower. Want to wager it was a cold one?

I tuned back in to Lana, who was still ranting, her voice rising to a pitch that made me want to run outside and jump in front of traffic.

"Slow down," I said. "As you can hear, I'm fine. How did you find out?"

"I saw it on the news. The report says the motel blew a few hours ago, and you didn't call."

Code for: Bitch, I was worried.

"Sorry about that. I was kind of busy." Getting my girl rocks off. Jiminy Cricket, that man had some talent.

Kind of made me excited for the sleeping situation. I'd noticed there was only one possible bed for us to share, and I could not wait to crawl into it as soon as I got off the phone. Which took almost two hours given Lana was on a roll. By the time I hung up and entered his bedroom, it was to find him already asleep.

Lucky for me, he took over only one half of the bed, an obvious invitation. I stripped before I crawled in beside him and snuggled. His arm came around me, tucking me closer, and I sighed.

This was awesome.

CHAPTER 9

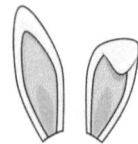

Awesome was waking up beside the woman he'd pleasured the night before. Less great was the fact he'd fallen asleep. However, whacking off in the shower, then listening to her argue with her friend, proved to be enough to lull him.

While Derek had partially awoken when she slid into bed with him, it didn't feel like the right time to start something. Besides, there was something to be said about her warm body close to his.

Trusting him.

Did he really want to move things too fast and scare her away?

Nope. Which was why, when he woke up, he took things slow... stroking his hand up and down her arm, lightly brushing her skin. She lay sprawled half atop him, her leg flung over his, her hand on his heart while her head was cradled in the crook of his arm and body.

She stirred, a soft sigh exhaling from her. She squirmed some more, her leg hiking more fully against him, the heat of her mound against his thigh. Rubbing.

Yes, she gyrated in her sleep against him.

The sheet tented over his groin.

"Morning," she mumbled against his skin.

"Morning, Enny. How did you sleep?"

"Let's just say I'm feeling a tad frisky this morning." Her hand slid down his bare chest to the waistband of his pants then skimmed lower until she could grip him, the loose fabric molding to his cock.

"Need me to help with your frisky problem?" he teased.

"I've got this." She rolled atop him, hands splayed on his chest, her legs straddling his body. Her buttocks pushed back and rubbed against his erection.

He palmed her waist, noticing she'd chosen to wear one of his shirts to bed. It looked good on her. But it would look even better on the floor. He slid his hands under the hem and touched her bare skin.

Might as well have stuck his hand in a fire. The heat of her skin scorched. She leaned down, but rather than kiss him, she nuzzled his neck. Soft, light pecks.

He reached and cupped her ass, noting she wore a thong rather than a full-bottom panty. Nice. It meant he kneaded bare flesh. It also meant the thin, wet crotch of them rubbed against his bare belly. The honeyed scent of her arousal teased him.

He slid a hand between her legs, still remembering how she'd felt coming on his fingers the night before. How she'd cried out his name. He touched her, and she gasped.

The slickness of her sex showed him how ready she was.

She lifted herself and reached down, gripping the waistband of his pants. She slowly began to tug and—

Bang. Bang. Bang.

"Are you fucking kidding me?" he growled as someone pounded his door.

"Think they brought breakfast?" she asked as she rolled off him, putting an obvious end to his possible morning meal.

"I'll be cooking their ass over a flame in a second, never fear." He jumped out of bed and stalked to the front door, his erection deflating rapidly the more his irritation grew. Who the hell was it?

He flung open the door and came face to face with a guy holding a huge box. "What is that? I didn't order anything."

"It's for a Claire Mahoney."

"Ooh, it's for me!" She emerged from the bedroom wearing his oversized shirt, which hit her mid-thigh, and nothing else, her hair rumpled, lips pink, and looking adorable.

The delivery dude noticed.

Derek growled.

The package got shoved at him, and the fellow practically ran off.

"My stuff! Lana must have super-express posted it." Claire grabbed the package, leaving Derek to slam the door shut.

He followed her into the living room in the hopes they'd continue what they'd started, only to see Claire tearing open the cardboard box and yanking out clothes. And a wad of cash. And more clothes. And chocolate bars.

"Does your roommate not realize we have stores here?"

"But none of them have Baby Ruth. Damn those Canadian tariffs for blocking my favorite treat." She tore one open and chewed off a chunk, closing her eyes and giving a happy hum.

"Shouldn't you have dessert after breakfast?"

She eyed him and smiled. "Is this a hint about eating a sausage first?"

The erection returned.

So, of course, her phone rang.

Then his phone rang. The fates conspired against him this morning. Since she was busy talking to her friend again, he answered.

It was a guy from work wanting him to take his shift. He was about to refuse, only Claire shook her head. *Take it*, she mouthed.

Only when he hung up did he say, "Why do you want me going in to work?"

"Because you're going to sneak me in with you. I want a peek around."

"No."

"Why not?"

"Because it's not a good idea."

"But I thought you said Chymera wasn't doing anything hinky."

"They're not."

"Then who cares if I poke around?"

"I do. If someone sees you, then you could get in trouble and I will probably get fired."

"Only if I'm caught. It's Sunday. I doubt there will be that many people."

Good point, but still not a good idea. Neither was leaving her unprotected in his house. "You can come, but you're sticking close to me."

"If you insist." She rose from the floor and moved close to him. "Is this close enough?"

He grabbed her around the waist and hauled her closer. "This is better."

Her lips quirked. "I didn't take you for the possessive type."

"I'm not usually. But there's something about you..." He brushed her cheek with his knuckle.

She leaned into the caress. "I feel the same way. Does this mean you want us to go steady?"

His turn to smile. "It's what would have happened in high school had you stuck around."

"Were you really going to ask me to be your girlfriend?"

"Yeah." He almost blushed at the fact they were talking about it, as if they were teenagers still.

"I would have said yes." She leaned up on tiptoe and brushed her mouth over his. "I still would." Then she twirled away from him until she was behind and slapped his ass. "Get those cheeks moving, Spot. You have to get to work."

"Spot?"

"I always wanted a dog, but my dad wouldn't let me have a pet. Not even a cat."

"Still doesn't explain Spot."

"Would you prefer Rufus? Duke?"

"How about none of the above?"

"Not fair. You gave me a nickname." The jutting lower lip was more than he could resist.

"Fine," he sighed. "If you must. But can you at least make it something cool?"

"Mad Max."

"I'm not rabid."

"Scooby?"

"I don't solve mysteries."

She planted her hands on her hips. "You're being difficult. You didn't see me arguing about the nickname you gave me."

"Because it's cute."

"So you want a cute name?" Her nose wrinkled.

"Can we go for something masculine? Strong?"

"Like Hercules or Zeus?"

Again, he couldn't help but shake his head. "A Greek god?"

Her lips twitched. "You're right, I've seen the statues. You're definitely better endowed, Big."

He almost blushed, even as his chest swelled. A man did like his attributes to be noticed.

His phone buzzed again, and a glance at the screen tightened his jaw.

"What's wrong?"

"Nothing."

"Don't tell me nothing. You look like someone kicked you in the schnitzels."

"Just something I've got to deal with."

Before he could tuck away his phone, she'd darted in and snatched it. Read the message. Turned a glare on him.

"What's this?" she said, pointing to the text notification box on his screen.

"A message."

"From my dad," she squeaked. "You told him I was here."

"Well, yeah."

"But I didn't say you could."

"You also didn't say I couldn't," he retorted.

"It was implied."

"Sorry. He's been worried sick about you. I thought I was doing the right thing telling him."

"The right thing?" She held up his phone. "This says, 'D, maybe you should just tie her up and bring her home. I'll deal with the fallout.'"

"He said it. Not me."

"And are you going to obey?" she sassed. "You going to take me back to your alpha like a good pack wolf?"

Why him? Why now? What happened to the awesome morning that had begun so well and devolved so rapidly?

"As a matter of fact, no, I wasn't. I'm not into kidnapping women, even stubborn ones who should have left town."

"You want me to leave. Then fine. I'll leave." She tossed him the phone. "I'm not going back."

He barred the door. "Don't go."

"You didn't exactly leave me a choice. You know why I left. Why I can't return."

"I know why you ran off, but I don't agree with it, just like I don't agree with the fact you can't go back. Your parents miss you."

Judging by the sudden tremble in her lips, she missed them, too, but she couldn't admit it. "I can't, Big. Please..." Tears shimmered, making him feel like the biggest asshole ever.

He sighed. "I won't force you. I might not like it, but I will respect your choice."

"Promise you won't tell my dad anything more about me."

He pressed his lips tight.

She placed her hand on his chest. "Please, Big, promise me."

How could he resist? "I promise. Jeezus." He scrubbed a hand through his hair. "I gotta shower if I'm gonna make it to work on time."

He left her before he made any more impossible promises. How the hell would he handle this? Could he really betray his alpha? But at the same time, how could he refuse her?

He put the shower on hot and steaming. The kind of heat that should melt away his troubles. He braced his palms on the wall, head hanging down, letting it stream over him.

The rustle of the curtain was his only warning before she touched him. He sucked in a breath.

Looked down and saw her kneeling in front of him.

"What are you doing?" His voice emerged gruff.

"Isn't it your turn?" she said, her gaze meeting his, her hair slicked back by the shower.

A man had only so much willpower. He didn't have any to push her away or say no. Not when her hand wrapped around his cock and held him tight. He managed only a strangled groan as her lips covered the head of his dick and sucked.

With his hands braced, his hips rocked in time to

the sweet suction of her mouth. He pulsed within her firm grip. She needed both hands to cover him, and her mouth could take only about two inches, but he didn't care. She was touching him. Pleasuring him. Humming her enjoyment as she sucked him.

And when he growled, "I'm going to come," she took it all, every last drop before releasing him with a wet pop.

Before he could recover and return the favor, she'd slipped away, stolen his only clean towel, and had breakfast cooking by the time he managed to dry off—with a face cloth—and dress.

"Thank you," he said. Not just for the eggs and bacon she placed in front of him with the most beautifully golden-brown hash.

She smiled. "You're welcome. Now hurry up. We don't want to be late for work."

We. Shit. She was coming with him.

The good news? He'd at least have her nearby to watch over.

The bad? He'd probably end up fired.

But watching her across the table, shoveling food and happily chatting about her friend Lana, who apparently had sent her a text of an ultrasound showing her baby almost full term, he didn't care.

He'd do anything to have her across the table from him every morning.

CHAPTER 10

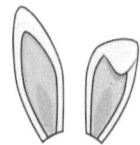

SINCE DEREK WASN'T ALLOWED to bring anyone to work with him, I got to hide in the back of his truck. Under a tarp. Which smelled of oil. Ew.

I'd much rather be smelling Derek. The man oozed yumminess, and it had nothing to do with sugar and chocolate but everything to do with desire.

He'd made me come. Hard. On his fingers. He'd left a good-sized hickey on my neck, which I am not ashamed to admit I wore as a badge of honor. I could almost taste his frustration at the interruptions that morning. It was part of the reason why I joined him in the shower.

The man deserved something because I could see how much giving me his word cost. Derek was a loyal pack member, but he was also a man of his word. If he promised to not spill anything more to my dad about me, then I knew I could trust him. Which said a lot about him given my request was unfair. A wolf had a duty to his alpha, but I couldn't deal with my family right now. Not yet. Maybe not ever.

Seeing the message hurt. Not because Derek had spilled the beans and told my dad he'd seen me but because the text clearly indicated my dad wanted me home.

Why? I was still the same bunny misfit who'd left. Surely everyone was better off with me gone?

Dwelling on it made me unhappy, and I didn't do misery. So I concentrated on something much nicer. Like Derek.

Problem was thinking of him soaked the crotch of my clean panties. I'd wanted nothing more than to jump his big bone that morning, but I couldn't let the possibility of epic sex get in the way of my mission. Lana was getting antsy. While I couldn't hide the motel blowing up, I could explain it as being an accident. Someone being careless with a cigarette. I didn't dare mention the kidnapping. She'd have had me yanked home so quick my head would spin.

I wasn't ready to go home. Not when I was having so much fun.

Yes, fun, and the blame belonged to Derek. I experienced a certain giddy pleasure in hearing Derek say he'd once upon a time planned to ask me to be his girlfriend.

Did anyone hear my inner squeal of delight?

Even more astonishing, he seemed intent on

making the past the present. In other words, I was pretty sure he was hinting that we date.

Or was that just nostalgia talking?

For all I knew, nostalgia was to blame for my feelings for him. From the moment I'd set eyes on him, I was sixteen all over again with my heart racing and my girl parts tingling.

Could we make a go of it? Sure, we got along now—and the make-out sessions were epic—but it had been not even two days since we met. Who was to say we'd even like each other after a week or a month? The novelty would eventually wear off. I'd try and make him eat more salads and slap his hand if it touched my chocolate stash during shark week.

He'd want to go home at Christmas and see his family, and I...I was a big fat chicken who had waited too long to have any chance to make amends.

Perhaps, had I done something within the first few years, I could have repaired the damage. But a decade?

Despite the message I'd seen, I remained convinced my family hated me by now. If they thought of me at all—because I wasn't sure they did, text or not. Could be they'd not thought of me in years until Derek mentioned seeing me.

They'd soon forget again.

The truck eventually stopped bouncing around, which was good because I almost tossed my cookies. Literally. I opened the bag, and a giant lurch sent a few flying. I rescued them, being a proud supporter of the ten-second rule.

When the truck slowed and did the whole back and forth thing as it parked, I knew better than to move. We'd discussed this beforehand. Derek would check things out and make sure it was safe first. Then I'd sneak out of the bed of the truck and do my stealthy best to not get caught. If I did, the excuse was I'd come to surprise my boyfriend with lunch, which I had stashed in my fanny pack—along with some toffees because I was pretty sure he had a sweet tooth. He just didn't know it yet.

He tapped the side of the truck, our signal. But I waited another sixty seconds—an eternity in bunny years—before I dared peek out from under the tarp.

No one yelled. I eased out farther and quickly hopped over the side, landing on the pavement in the shadow of a tree. He'd parked at the edge of the lot to give us more cover.

I took a moment to breathe in the air. Fading exhaust. A hint of garbage from the dumpster about twenty yards away. Foliage from the forest edging the lot. And cigarette smoke.

Which was odd because I didn't see anyone.

What I didn't smell? Nefarious plots. Kind of disappointing given my certainty evil had a specific stench.

I kept to the trees as I approached the main building of Chymera. While Derek remained convinced it was on the up and up, I had my doubts. If they were so clean and aboveboard, why did he try so hard to keep me away?

Maybe so he doesn't get fired. I could almost hear Lana and her logical reasoning for everything.

But I could also play the game of what-if.

What if he didn't want me here because he was hiding something?

What if he was part of the devious goings on?

What if he lied to me and had a girlfriend who worked here, and he was afraid we'd run into each other, and then he'd be caught and in so much trouble?

If that were true, then I seriously needed help when it came to gauging people.

In this case, I trusted my bunny sense. Derek wasn't a bad person. Perhaps he truly missed all the clues pointing to this workplace being a super-secret installation involved in the kidnapping and experimenting of supers.

I'd have to bring him proof.

With that determination, I slunk around the building. I sniffed out every corner. I shed a silent tear at the half-eaten chocolate bar tossed to the ground and covered in an army of ants.

What kind of monsters worked here!

I peeked in windows. Even managed to slip inside because someone left a back door wedged open when they wandered out for a smoke. I ghosted through as many halls and rooms as I could. Many of them were locked. Those that weren't were boring. Worst of all, I smelled only humans.

Could I be wrong? Perish the thought.

Exiting the building, I made my way back to the guardhouse, sneaky as could be. The building, which was about ten by ten—making it bigger than my first apartment—had only one door in the front. But the window in the back worked well enough for me, especially since I heard Derek talking to someone in an idling car.

I dumped myself into his office and crawled under his desk, wrinkling my nose as more of that cigarette smoke filled the room. How rude of the idling driver to puff while dealing with Derek.

A moment later, the engine noise receded and there was a creak as Derek sat in the chair. He drummed his fingers on his desk, not once looking under it.

Since I wasn't the type to be ignored, I grabbed him by the crotch.

He yelled, "What the fuck!" and I poked my head out.

"Hey, Big. Did I scare you?"

"Yeah you fucking scared me."

"I thought wolves had a super sense of smell."

"We do for new scents, but given you rubbed yourself all over me before I started my shift, I kind of figured it was a lingering effect."

I kind of liked the idea of him wearing my aroma. It might warn others away from him. Mine. All mine. A fantasy I indulged in for a second.

"What are you doing under there?"

"Having fun?" I said on a high note.

"Seriously."

"Being discreet like you asked."

"Get out of there."

"I thought I was supposed to stay hidden."

"You're good for now. The place is empty. That was the last person checking out. So unless someone comes up the road, we're alone. Did you find anything?"

"No." My lips turned down. "Not even a mutant spider."

"Told you Chymera was on the up and up."

"And I'm telling you there's got to be something happening around here somewhere. Is there another building maybe?"

"Not that I've seen. Nor are there any trails in the woods before you ask."

"But you said they own tons of land."

"They do."

"Then there could be a secret installation somewhere else."

"Why are you so determined to find something?" he asked.

"It's not for me, but my friend. Lana." Since we had time to kill, and he guarded his crotch and said not while on the job, I told him the whole story. Every ugly bit about my best friend, Beth, who was dying of a childhood illness until they injected her with demon and angel blood, turning her into a hybrid. With a destiny.

Then he got Lana's sad tale, being raised for the first years of her life in some kind of military bunker until her adopted mom helped her escape. He didn't say a word as I told him about Lana's discovery that her birth mom was a Siren named Bella and her dad, Neptune himself. Both missing, presumed either dead or captive.

By the end of my story, his expression was pensive—and sexy. "So you're looking for Neptune?"

I nodded my head.

"What makes you think he's here?"

I told him about the video and the coffee cup.

His head dipped. He sighed. Drummed his fingers.

"What's wrong, Big?"

"What's wrong is I can't lie to you. There is a secret installation."

"What?" I yelled. Not entirely surprised. I'd known he was holding back.

"Before you get mad, I didn't want to tell you because I really would prefer you leave town. I wasn't joking about it being dangerous here."

"Because this is the place. This is where they're experimenting on our kind."

"Maybe. I don't know for sure. Which is why I was sent here."

"Who sent you?" Only to answer my own question. "Daddy sent you."

"Not specifically. Me and a bunch of other guys joined the temp agency that Chymera uses to find staff. The agency sent me here to work."

"And you report what you find back to my dad," I said aloud. "This means the pack knows what's happening."

"Not exactly. But we knew something was up. Over the past few years, people have gone missing. All shifters. No bodies ever found."

"Why didn't you tell me?" I couldn't help the hurt in my tone. I'd been honest with him. I couldn't believe he'd been lying to me.

"Because I wanted to keep you out of it."

"Wanted to protect me because I'm a weak bunny who can't take care of herself," I huffed.

When I would have moved, he grabbed me and yanked me into his lap. "Because I care about you and I didn't want to see you hurt. After the kidnapping attempt, do you know how hard it was to go home? I just wanted to sleep outside your door."

"Why didn't you?" I asked. "After all, his accomplice could have come back."

"Because I knew you'd hate it. That first night we ran into each other, you made it clear you're all about standing on your own two feet. Which I respect. It means I can't mollycoddle you even if it almost kills me to walk away."

"But you followed me that first night. You didn't think I could walk home alone."

"I followed you so I'd know where you were staying. How else could I have seen you again?" His lips tilted.

"You should have been smarter and stolen my wallet."

"Apparently not all of us are as gifted in five-finger borrowing as you are."

I laughed. "Not all that gifted considering I was groping you pretty noticeably when I took it."

"I'm sorry I lied to you." His face turned serious.

"Can't really be mad, I guess. You were also on a mission. The good news is now we can work together. Starting with, where the heck is this secret installation?"

"Somewhere in the acreage behind the institute."

"So you don't know where it is?"

He shook his head. "Not exactly. And again, this is only an assumption. About a week or so ago, on a secondary road leading out of this place, I spotted an off-road track going into the woods. It seemed kind of curious, so I parked and went for a walk. I didn't get far before some dude stopped me and told me I was trespassing."

"Human I assume?"

"He seemed to be, but I couldn't be sure because the guy had no scent."

"Impossible. Everyone has a smell."

"Exactly. But he didn't, and that's how he snuck up on me. I never even knew he was there until he spoke."

"Did you pee yourself?" I asked. "That happened to me once. I had to really go, and I was walking into the apartment and Lana, my roommate, screamed 'Boo,' and I yelled and sneezed at the same time. It wasn't pretty."

Again, he got the strangest look on his face.

"You know, most people would keep that story to themselves."

"There are many things in my life I have to keep secret. Embarrassing moments aren't one of them." Besides, maybe if he thought of me as a girl who peed her pants he'd stop looking at me in that smoldering way that told my panties to take a hike. We had serious business to discuss that wouldn't get done if my mouth was full of his penis.

"Back to the point of the story. Whatever is in those woods is guarded by people we can't smell coming."

"Have you told anyone?"

"Not yet. See, I happened to meet an old friend, and things got kind of crazy."

I found it rather flattering that I distracted him.

Bunny Misfit

Now, however, was time to focus. "We need to go back to that road you found."

"Obviously, but the problem remains: How do we reach whatever is in those woods?"

"I can reach it."

"How? The guard will stop us the minute they find us trespassing." Him and his logic.

"Which is why we'll have to make sure we're not spotted. Good thing the full moon is tomorrow night."

His eyes widened. "Oh hell no. You can't take your bunny in there."

"Why not?"

"Because you're a rabbit, Enny. And rabbits aren't exactly fearsome predators who can take out guards."

"One, that's a rather broad assumption to make." Not to mention my bunny was not as useless as he thought. "And two, why take out a guard if I can sneak by him?"

"Sneak?" He snickered. "Enny, it might have been years since I saw your rabbit, but some things can't be forgotten. As I recall, you are freaking huge."

"Are you calling my bunny fat?" I angled my chin.

"Not fat, but definitely oversized. You're what, a hundred pounds?"

"Hundred and five."

"Even compacted, that's a one-hundred-and-five-pound rabbit. The world's largest known species is the continental giant, and the biggest one on record is only fifty-five pounds. You're almost twice that size."

"How do you know that?"

He shrugged and wouldn't look me in the eye. His head ducked, and he practically blushed as he mumbled, "I might have read up on rabbits after you turned into one."

"Why?"

"Because I wanted to know more about them."

"Again, why?"

He finally raised his head enough to stare me in the eyes. "Because I used to like this girl who turned into one."

"Used to?" I found myself utterly fascinated by the conversation, by the fact this guy I used to crush on had taken the time to do research, because of me.

"Yeah, used to. Because she ran away without a word or a goodbye and never came back."

The rebuke stung, and I defended myself. "I didn't want to be a burden on the pack."

"Did it ever occur to you that you caused a bigger burden to those you left behind?"

To my shame, I'd always assumed everyone felt relief. Even my parents. After all, I was an embarrassment to the two strongest people in our pack. Surely, despite their claim they loved me still, they were better off without a broken daughter?

"I thought I was doing the right thing." Which sounded lame even to my ears.

And he didn't spare me any quarter. "No, it wasn't the right thing. You were a selfish asshole. Good news, though, there's still time to apologize for it."

I grimaced. "You want me to talk to my parents. I thought we already discussed the fact I wasn't interested."

"Yeah, I know you're not. Doesn't mean it's the right choice."

"You promised you wouldn't bring me home."

"And I'll keep that promise, even if it's a dumb one."

"You calling me a dumb bunny?"

"If the stubborn fits." He held my gaze. "Listen, Enny, I know you're scared. But I think if you just talked to them. Hell, maybe if you saw them... Maybe you'd see there's nothing to be frightened of."

See them? My heart fluttered, and my hands shook. I shoved myself from his lap and paced. "I can't."

His hands anchored themselves to my arms and forced me to stop. "Calm down."

"I'm calm."

"No, you're not. I can hear your heart racing. Why are you so frightened? It's your mom and dad. They love you."

"Do they?" I tilted my face. "I'm not their perfect

daughter anymore. My dad even wondered if I was his." The DNA tests run on me afterwards to see why I was the way I was proved otherwise. However, all the tests in the world couldn't fix me.

"They had a shock, and maybe they didn't handle it as well as they should have. But you never gave them a chance to apologize. Never gave them a chance to get to know the new you."

"I was a freaking bunny in a pack of wolves. I didn't have time. I was too worried about getting eaten."

"In time the pack would have accepted you."

I scowled. "You don't know that for sure."

"Neither do you because you ran before giving anyone a chance."

"Fine. I get it. I was a jerk who should have tried a little harder. Enough with the guilt trip. You are totally being a downer." Which made me crave chocolate something fierce.

I got something sweeter as he held me tight and pulled me closer.

"I'm sorry, Enny. Don't be mad." His lips brushed my temple, then my cheek, before finding my mouth. I melted into him and might have taken him right there on his rickety desk except we heard a car coming.

"Shit. Can you duck out of sight?"

I did one better. I dove out the window. With his

keys. Things were getting complicated, and I needed something with icing to help calm me down.

As he was bent down dealing with the person coming in, I raced out with his truck. Not stealing, merely borrowing it for a bit. I blew him a kiss as I went by and shouted, "Pick you up at five."

I drove into town and hit the grocery store. Super excited to see my favorite brand of ice cream on sale. What I didn't expect was to also bring home a man.

Not that I told Derek about our visitor when I picked him up at the end of his shift.

Boy was Derek surprised when he walked in the door, wearing a scowl, and saw our guest tied to a chair.

"Um, Enny, what the fuck?"

"Remember how you said we needed a cover to get in?"

"Yeah."

"I found it."

CHAPTER 11

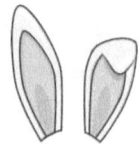

As PLANS WENT, hers wasn't the worst he'd heard of, but that didn't stop Derek from pacing.

"Let me get this straight," he said, pivoting before he hit the wall. "You went to the grocery store for junk food."

"I don't know if I'd call it junk. Ambrosia of the gods seems like a better title."

"And you happened to see this guy?"

"Not just any guy." Claire pointed to her captive. "Check it out, I found Igor, the same fellow who tried to kidnap me."

Igor glared in reply.

It took Derek a moment to process her claim. "Did you say Igor? Is that really his name?"

"Um, no, I kind of made it up on account he has no wallet. I checked."

This time he blinked. Confused about the fact he was angry. "You went through his pockets?"

"All of them, even the tiny change one. But don't worry, he didn't enjoy it one bit, so no need to be jealous."

"I'm not jealous." He was pissed. The reason? She'd touched another guy. *Shit, I am jealous.* Not that he said anything out loud. She didn't need more ammo.

Claire approached him and placed her hands on his chest, peeking up at him with utmost seriousness. "I would never cheat on you, Big. Especially now that we're kind of an item."

"Are we?" For some reason this did much to soothe the irritation. Until he looked at the man in the chair. He wouldn't be enjoying any of the benefits that came with them being an item with Igor in his house.

That brought about a long sigh. "Let's go back to the part where you saw your kidnapper. Of course, your first thought wasn't to get away but to abduct him instead."

"I know, brilliant, right? And ironic. He kidnapped me, I kidnapped him." She beamed. "So any-hoo, I happened to drive around the back of the grocery store—"

"Because the long way out of the parking lot is great for gas consumption."

"—when I saw the delivery van parked by a loading dock. The same van that's been picking up huge grocery orders every few days."

"Which is suspicious," he said sarcastically.

"Well yeah. I mean who needs that much raw fish, meat, and vegetables? The thirty pounds of carrots, I get. Great snack with loads of vitamin C. But did you know there wasn't even a single box of cookies in there?"

"A true crime."

She nodded. "No kidding because everyone knows sugar is needed for true happiness."

"I didn't know that." Although, given how he felt in the moment, he began to suspect what he needed—ahem, who—in order to find his happy place.

"When I saw Igor was the guy behind the wheel, I knew right away I had to steal his van."

"You stole it with him in it," Derek stated flatly.

"I did." She sounded so proud of herself. "After I knocked him out—"

"With a tire iron?"

Her bouncy hair whipped back and forth. "Nope. Couldn't find one in your truck, which is a bad idea. What if you get a flat tire?"

"I call a tow truck." Because his spare had a hole, too.

"Since you didn't have anything I could use as a whacking stick, I had to improvise. I jumped in the back of the van when Igor wasn't looking, and when he sat in the driver's seat, I put him in a sleeper hold."

"That doesn't actually work." A cool-looking

wrestling move but almost impossible to accomplish. Especially given her size versus Igor's.

"It does too work if you jam a plastic bag over their head first."

He shook his head in disbelief. "Remind me to never piss you off."

"Keep making my panties wet and we'll be fine." Only as she blushed did he realize she'd said more than she intended.

Did his cock get hard? Fucking right it did. But he couldn't concentrate on that fact right now. Because there was something he needed to clarify. "Um, where is his van?" Because she'd picked Derek up in his truck.

"I parked it a few blocks away from the grocery store in the alley behind the strip club. Then moved him from the van to your truck to here. Tada." She gestured and beamed.

"How the hell did you move him? He outweighs you by at least fifty pounds. Did you have help?"

"I'm stronger than I look." Said with a wink.

"Were you seen?" Should he worry the police were about to raid his home and charge him as an accomplice?

She blew a raspberry. "P-l-le-ease. I am not a dumb bunny."

"Just a rash one. What you did was dangerous. This whole thing was a bad idea, Enny."

"Bad how? Instead of waiting for tomorrow night

for the full moon and infiltrating in bunny stealth mode, I got us a Trojan van."

He shook his head. "First off, we have no idea where that van was going. Maybe it's for an old age home or a commune out in the boonies. We don't even know Igor works for them."

She jabbed her finger at Igor. "He tried to kidnap me."

"And? Could be he's a *Silence of the Lambs* kind of guy." After all, she was tasty looking. "The point is we don't know for sure what his motive was because I doubt Igor told you anything."

"He's been a little shy about communicating," she admitted, rubbing her toe on the floor and looking adorably chagrinned.

"Could it be because you have tape over his mouth?"

"I didn't have a choice," she explained. "He was using some really foul language. My ears were burning."

"You can't go around kidnapping people, Enny."

"He did it first." She stamped her foot in irritation. "Which makes us even."

"Except for the fact you escaped and he's still in my house."

"You want me to untie him?" She moved around to the back of Igor, and Derek yelled, "No."

Not because he didn't think he could handle the big guy. Igor was human, and wolf beat them every day no matter the size. "We don't need him calling his bosses and telling them we're onto their crimes."

"Right." She nodded. "We need to keep him prisoner until we've found the secret base, called in the troops, and evil is vanquished once and for all."

"You have a vivid fantasy life, don't you?"

"Yes, and you should see the outfits for some of it." She winked.

Given how little blood remained in his brain, he was close to not caring if Igor was tied in his living room. He had to ignore the distraction.

Derek turned away from her and mulled over the problems with her plan. "Let's say the van is involved and we take it on that dirt road. There will be guards. They won't just let us drive in. Once they stop us, they'll realize we're not the regular drivers."

"Not much I can do about that unless you're a master of disguise like that Cruise fellow in those Bourne movies."

"That's *Mission Impossible*, which is an apt description for what you're suggesting. We're going to be caught."

"You might, but they won't keep you captive for long. While you're distracting the guards at the gate, I will slip in, make sure we've got the right place, and then lead the cavalry to the spot."

"What if they shoot me?"

Her turn to flutter her lashes. "Why would they do that?" Asked most guilelessly.

"You say these people think nothing of capturing our kind and experimenting on us. What makes you think they won't just shoot me on sight?"

"Because you're going to show them some teeth. That will show your value. They won't dare shoot you then."

"I am not shifting." He was adamant on that point.

"Then you better hope they don't aim to kill."

He gritted his teeth. "I have a better idea. Why don't I make some calls? Get some backup. Raid this place with actual people trained for this kind of thing."

"You are not calling my dad," she yelled, no longer smiling and very agitated.

"We have to call someone."

"I told you, I've got that covered. And besides, we can't wait for anyone to arrive. The bad guys will realize something is wrong when Igor doesn't show with the goods."

He pointed out the flaw in her plan. "Don't you think they'll have noticed that by now?"

A sly smile graced her lips. "Why do you think I parked the van by the strip club? Igor apparently likes to support the local single mothers with his ill-earned gains."

"The groceries though..."

"The perishable items are packed in ice."

He rubbed his chin and paced some more. "This is crazy, Enny."

"It's the break I've been looking for. But if you're too scared—"

The look he shot her bordered on a glare. "I'm not scared. Worried we'll get killed? Yes. You and me, that's only two people. And neither of us with a gun."

"We don't need no stinkin' guns," she boasted, looking about as dangerous as that chipmunk shaking a nut at him last fall.

"We should call someone, let them know what we're planning."

"If it makes you feel better, I'll tell Lana to send the Vikings. But they will be a few hours. The closest they can get is Calgary."

"Where are they flying in from?"

"More like with who. They're coming on the Genie Express."

"What?"

She grinned. "Magic, Big. They're gonna get teleported there."

He closed his eyes and sighed. "Why me?"

"Because you're the luckiest man alive."

"Not for long." Because if this crazy plan failed he might be pushing up daisies by the morning.

But if it succeeded... He'd make sure to celebrate with Claire in bed.

CHAPTER 12

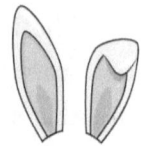

I HID in the back of the van—munching on some carrots—Igor bound beside me amidst the roast beef and pork tenderloin. In the driver's seat, Derek wore a ball cap and a bulky sweater, doing his best to beef up his appearance.

It wouldn't work, but I didn't say that. He already had enough doubts about my epic plan.

On the drive in, I tried to distract him. "How attached are you to your job here?"

"Why?" he asked.

Because two days of Derek had me thinking ahead. Crazy. I know. But he made me feel things. And not just when his fingers were inside me.

He knew who I was. The new me, and the old me. Even the bunny me. He liked what he saw. Heck, he liked me enough to not freak out at the man trussed like a turkey in his living room and then, despite his grumbling, drove off into the dark and unknown looking for a dirt road in the woods.

So when he asked why I was questioning his job, I told him the truth. "I'd like you to meet my friends." A huge step. Very few guys in our lives ever merited that honor. We didn't want to waste time and energy with a fellow who wasn't the "one." Or in Beth's case, the "two."

"I'm sure I can get some time off," he hedged. "But my family will be expecting me to go back home at one point."

I pursed my lips. That could be a problem. "I guess we could do shared custody."

He choked.

I pounded him on the back and laughed. "Don't die. I'm just kidding. Forget what I said. I mean, it's obvious that once this mission is over, we'll have to break up."

"What?" The van swerved.

"I was crazy to think it would go any further. I mean, you're great and all, like super great, but—"

He slammed the van to a stop and turned to face me. "Listen. I like you a lot, too, and I'll be the first to admit I don't know where we'll end up. But I can tell you one thing. No matter what happens tonight, I want to see you tomorrow and the next day. Probably for a long while. And if you're not ready to go home, your real home, and see your family, then we'll figure something out."

"We will?" An optimistic note in my voice.

"We will." A firm statement. "If we don't die tonight."

I leaned forward and gave him a kiss. "We won't die. End up in a cage and forced to breed to make babies, possibly. Strapped to a table donating blood and tissue, also possible. But killing us would be a waste."

"That wasn't reassuring," he grumbled, facing forward again and lurching the van into motion.

"I won't let anything happen to you, Big." Not after he'd admitted he liked me.

I leaned close to Igor and whispered, "He likes me."

That was better than chocolate.

Igor didn't reply, probably on account he was sad that his chances of turning to good and wooing me had just evaporated. That and the tape still over his mouth.

The van slowed and turned, transitioning from smooth pavement to the jostling roughness of a dirt road. Most of the groceries sat in boxes for easy transport. The bushel of apples stayed upright, but at a good bump, a few stray ones went flying and rolling. One landed right in my mouth. How fortuitous since I needed a sweet snack.

Derek grumbled in the front. "There are cameras in the trees."

"We're totally in the right place."

"We should have waited for backup." He was worried.

I forgave him because I was a teeny tiny bit scared, too. I'd never done anything this bold and daring before. My inner bunny twitched, urging flight. Despite the trepidation, though, I also thrummed with excitement. At long last, I understood the appeal of adrenaline. The more I conquered my fear and acted, the more I craved.

Tonight was the ultimate adrenaline stunt. I was about to infiltrate a top-secret installation. Me, a floppy-eared bunny, was about to do something heroic.

Hooray for a misfit.

As for Derek's fear we'd fail?

Not happening, because I had plans for later that involved the chocolate icing I'd bought and kisses. Lots of kisses. Which made me wonder how Derek would feel if I melted the chocolate over him and licked it off. It would solve two cravings at once.

The darkness pushed in all around the van, and despite driving in the woods, not a single branch scraped the sides. The indication of a path well worn by vehicles larger than this.

A few miles took forever—"It's been only three minutes since we left the road," said Derek—a lifetime in bunny years.

When he said, "I see lights," in a low voice, I hunkered down. This was the dangerous part of the plan. The part where he slowed down, I slipped open the side door, and jumped out. We'd already removed the bulb in the dome light so nobody could see.

But I had to time this right.

I yanked and dove, doing my best to shove the door back. Derek had lowered the window, and I could hear the tunes blare, muffling the click of the door shutting. Had to love those new electronic ones.

I paused in the underbrush as the van rolled on, listening for a yell. No one raised an alarm. Still, I knelt there frozen.

I can do this.

Bunnies aren't meant to be heroes, my inner friend reminded.

Tell that to Roger Rabbit and Bugs. I forced myself to my feet and kept to the cover of the trees. I flowed in the direction of the light, but at an angle. I doubted they'd fenced the whole place, but at the same time, I was conscious they probably had something in place to act as a perimeter warning.

My foot froze midair as my nose twitched.

Slowly, I peeked down. Noted the taut cable on the ground.

Ha. Spotted it.

I hopped over. Landed on something and had a moment to utter, "Fiddlesticks," before I was swept into the air.

CHAPTER 13

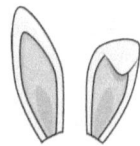

Derek knew he was screwed the moment he pulled to a stop by the guardhouse. Because lo and behold, there was his buddy, Sunglasses at Night. A cigarette dangled from his lips as Derek pulled to a stop.

"You're not Dave." The gun pointed at his face had only one reply.

"Dave's not here right now." A joke the guy obviously didn't get. Not many watched the Cheech and Chong classics. He'd wager Claire would find them immensely funny. Thinking of Claire reminded him he had to do his best to cause a distraction.

"Get out of the van." The gun never wavered as the demand was made.

For a moment, Derek pondered slamming the gas. Pedal to the metal. Where would he go? He wasn't bullet proof, and now that Sunglasses knew that he knew about the secret no one else knew, he'd probably end up dead even if he did manage to escape.

So, he decided to place faith in Claire's assertion that they'd prefer to take him alive. Derek exited the van, hands over his head, and smiled. Smiled with more teeth than he should.

Sunglasses flicked the cigarette to the side. "You call those teeth?" The guy finally removed his dark lenses and opened his mouth wide to show two sharp layers behind his human set. Freakiest of all was not his yellow lizard eyes but the fact—

"You have no scent."

"Because I'm not an animal like you," sneered the hybrid.

"What are you?" Derek asked, fascinated and appalled all at once.

"The future. Now move." The gun waved at him. "Or don't. I have no problem shooting you."

"Why are you doing this?" Derek asked, marching ahead.

"Doing what? Protecting company property? Because it's my job."

"I meant what's happening here. You're abducting and experimenting on people."

"People?" Sunglasses snorted. "The term they prefer to use is morph-capable creatures featuring genetic anomalies."

"Who is 'they'?"

"The scientists. The moneymen. Those looking forward to a better future."

"How is kidnapping folks and using them better?"

"They're taking their best traits and melding them to make something new."

"What if I don't want to be something new?"

Sunglasses chuckled. "Not you. You won't merit that kind of upgrade. You'll just provide genetic fodder."

A term that reminded him of what Claire said about being used for breeding. "Where are you taking me?"

"You'll see."

Derek did his best to look around and get details, but he was rather restricted in the sense that there wasn't much to see. Some bulky shapes that might be vehicles hidden under netting. A few storage sheds. They appeared headed straight for a rock wall.

A wall with a hidden door. Sunglasses pulled aside more camouflage netting and pressed his palm against a square pad. Without a sound, the door swung open, spilling light.

"After you."

Considering the smells wafting out didn't reassure, Derek hesitated, planting his feet firmly on the ground.

He didn't need his wolf's warning to know entering

was a bad idea. On the other hand, while Sunglasses might have a gun, he was also alone. Derek had seen no other soldiers. Didn't scent anyone either, which didn't mean shit. There could be a hundred like Sunglasses with no scent to detect, and he'd never know.

"Move." The barrel of the gun nudged him in the spine.

Don't go in there. Wasn't just his wolf that thought it was a bad idea. Despair flavored the air, but what cinched it was hearing a yodeled, "Peanut butter on saltine crackers. Let me down."

Claire needs me.

Derek whirled, and his fist lashed out, not aiming for the face as expected but rather for Sunglass's arm. The gun went off, the stray bullet missing Derek. He didn't wait for the guy to try again. Derek rushed him. Being close would make it harder to shoot. He grappled with Sunglasses, straining with the effort.

Along with teeth and freaky eyes, buddy had some epic strength.

Still, Derek had been a wolf a long time. A scrapper, too. He let a bit of the change envelope him. His claws extended while his teeth sharpened to points, and his jaw elongated to give him a wider bite radius.

Sunglasses matched him for partial shift, his skin taking on a scaly cast, his fingers growing talons that sank into skin.

It was fucking on.

Breaking free, Derek slugged the guy. Got a punch in the gut as a reply. A slash of claws and they were both bleeding.

A new voice shouted, "Tranq him. Boss says he wants him."

"We might hit Toby." A nasally hesitation.

"Fuck Toby," growled the first voice. "He could use a nap. Shoot."

Ah shit. Derek tried to duck so that only Toby took the shot. But he miscalculated. He felt the pinprick of a dart entering his skin. Immediately sluggishness filled his veins. He sank to his knees, losing his grip on Toby. But good news, Toby hit the ground with him. They both wavered, and Derek managed a slurred, "Fucker," before hitting the ground face first.

When he woke, it was to find himself pinned with someone cupping his groin and his traitor penis stirring.

He'd been captured, and they were already trying to breed him.

"No!" he snarled. "I won't be your rutting bull."

CHAPTER 14

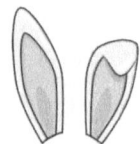

"Are you sure about that?" I whispered.

Immediately, Derek stopped bucking. "Enny, is that you?"

"In the flesh, Big." Just to prove it, I rubbed myself against him. At least this time he noticed. When they'd dumped him in my cell hours ago, he'd not reacted at all. He also snored.

I might have let him enjoy a nap, but we didn't have much time. Hence why when yelling, pinching, cajoling, and singing didn't work, I resorted to seduction.

Also known as groping.

Wouldn't you know, that woke him up.

"So I'm not a captive being used for breeding?" he said, sitting up, only to groan and lie back down. "Enny, is it me or are we in a cell?"

"We're in a cell. Inside a mountain, which explains why this place was so hard to find."

"How is it we're together?"

"For one, apparently they're running out of room. The kidnapping business has been good. And secondly, we are together because the creepy doctor who paid me a visit wants us to copulate."

That got his attention. He sat up again, and I rolled onto my back.

"What creepy doctor?"

"The one running the experiments here. Smile, Big, we did it. We found the place."

"Which does us no good since we're locked up."

"Oh, it could be worse."

"How?" he grumbled.

"They could have given us to other prisoners."

Had to love the way he stiffened and growled. Jealousy was sexier than expected.

"I am going to get us out of here." He rose and paced.

"You hiding a lockpick somewhere, Big?" I rolled to watch him on the mattress. A foam thing a few inches thick, set on the floor. The only thing positive I could say about it was it appeared new.

"How solid are these doors?" he asked, moving to it. He quickly realized he couldn't grab it by any seam. There weren't even any bars or a window, just a slim slot for food.

"Might as well come sit with me." I patted the bed.

"Sit?" he growled. "We're prisoners."

"For the moment. Have a little faith."

"How? No one knows we're here."

"Oh please. We both know you told my dad what we were doing."

"But I didn't tell him where. Just like your so-called cavalry has no idea we're in the mountain."

"They'll find us. I just hope they're quick about it."

He whirled. "Why?"

"Because I overheard Dr. Creepy say the lab was being moved. Apparently, they did notice me nosing around town, so they're closing up shop."

"When?"

"Soon. Before dawn if I overheard correctly."

"What?" Derek sat down beside me. "This isn't good, Enny. If they manage to move us, we won't be rescued, and I don't know how we'll escape."

"We'll escape. Don't forget, the full moon is coming."

"And?"

I smiled. "You let me worry about it." I patted his cheek.

He scowled.

I leaned in and kissed the frown from his lips.

He melted a tiny bit.

I kissed him again, slipping him some tongue.

"This." Smooch. "Isn't." A suck of his lip. "The time for this, Enny." He pulled back, and I pouted.

"Actually, there is no better time. You said it yourself, what if we're not rescued and we can't escape?" I leaned close. "Do you really want that to happen without having at least once made love to me?" I batted my lashes.

He stared at me. "Someone could interrupt."

"Then we'll make it quick."

"They could be watching."

I smiled. "Let them."

"I don't want anyone seeing you." That jealousy of his flared again.

I ran a finger down his cheek. "Then you'll have to find them and rip out their eyes."

"That shouldn't sound so sexy."

Straddling his lap, making him a prisoner of my desire, I whispered against his lips. "Take me, Big. Now."

He groaned against my mouth, his arms wrapping around me tight. My body pinned his, and despite the clothes we wore, there was no mistaking the hard nudge of his erection. It matched the aching in my pussy. I knew he was worried. Quite honestly, so was I. I wasn't lying when I said this could be our last chance.

Which meant I had to make this moment memorable. I caught his lips and sucked at the lower one, loving how ragged his breathing turned.

While we kissed, his hands skimmed my curves,

roaming from my back down to the indent of my waist. His fingers dug in for a moment when I ground my crotch against him.

"This is crazy, Enny." The groaned words only made my desire for him flare bright.

I bit his lip before going after his tongue, sucking it into my mouth, wanting the flavor of it. He kept touching me, running his hands over my hips then cupping my buttocks. Made me wish I'd worn a skirt. But nope. I'd worn pants, and they took a minute to strip. But because of his growl, I kept my panties on. I noticed his eyes trained on the red spot in the ceiling. He'd seen the camera.

He tried to protest. "We shouldn't. They're watching."

I cupped his face. "Then we'll make sure they don't see anything hardcore. Trust me."

"Claire." He sighed my name as I kissed him. He didn't push me away. Rather the palms of his hands cupped my butt, kneading the flesh.

I freed him from his pants—those evil things keeping us apart. Grasped him in my hand and he gasped.

But before I could move my panties aside for the main event, he was changing things up. He stood, hands still gripping my butt, and held me aloft. He moved until my back hit the wall.

It didn't take a genius to catch on to his plan. I

looped my arms around his shoulders, lifted my legs, and locked them around his waist.

The entire time we kissed, lips parted that our tongues might duel. I might have started out in control of the embrace, but he took over. Tasting me. Thrusting his tongue into my mouth for a sensuous exploration.

I'd never been so aroused. So...hungry. A part of me, a primal part I'd never seen before during sex, wanted me to bite him. To mark him.

Such an animal thing to do.

I chose instead to give him a hickey, sucking on the flesh of his neck.

His fingers pushed aside my panties, the bulk of his body hiding his actions from the camera.

He touched me, and I cried out. His fingers rubbed against my slick folds. I was more than ready for him.

He groaned. "I want to taste you so bad."

"What's stopping you?"

"An audience," he grumbled, his finger sliding in and out of me.

"This might be your only chance to ever taste me," I reminded.

He growled. "Fuck me, you know how to tease."

"You're the one teasing." I nipped at his ear lobe. "Now I can't stop wondering how good it would feel."

"Fuck it. Let them watch and envy me." He unhooked my legs, and I couldn't believe it.

He dropped to his knees.

I parted my thighs, and he let out a sound as he said, "Smells so fucking good."

He left my panties on. Some form of modesty, I guess. He pressed his mouth against the damp fabric, and I caught my breath. He sucked me, and I didn't care if there was a thin layer of silk between his mouth and my pussy, it felt so good.

My fingers dug into his scalp as I held him close to me, panting and moaning, the only words coming out of me being, "Yes. Oh. Yes."

When he finally pushed aside the fabric and truly placed his mouth on me I had a mini orgasm. My body shook, and I cried out. I continued to cry out as his tongue stroked my nether lips, spreading them that he might stab his tongue inside. To give him better access, I lifted a leg over his shoulder. In thanks, he paid attention to my clit.

I definitely shuddered hard at the touch, and I whispered his name, "Derek."

As for him? In between licks and sucks and hot, blowing breaths, he growled, the rumble against my sex incredible.

My body quivered, and I couldn't catch my breath as I got close to the edge. He stood, holding me upright. A good thing because I didn't think my legs could support me. His erection poked at my belly as I looped my arms around his neck. He lifted me high enough that it ended up under me, and I could wrap my legs around his waist.

The tip of him probed at the opening of my sex. He slowly slid in, the width of him stretching my channel. It felt incredible.

I grabbed his cheeks and drew him near for a kiss, wanting to be as close to him as possible.

Slowly, he began to thrust into me, rotating his hips to push deeper. Filling me. Claiming me. This was more than sex. I'd had sex. This...this transcended it. We were joined. Our bodies moving in rhythm, our pulses racing in time.

In and out, he thrust and ground, bringing me to a peak. As my orgasm hit, I gasped into his mouth, a sound he swallowed.

My climax rolled through my body, making me tense and pulse at the same time. He came with me, his hips driving deep one last time, his body going still as he came inside me.

Our bodies joined together.

As for our hearts... I leaned my forehead against his and said, "I think I love you more than chocolate."

Derek never got a chance to reply. The door to our cell was rudely yanked open.

My lover dropped me and turned to face the threat—with his penis hanging out. As for me, I was feeling kind of dazed. Not that being alert would have made a difference.

The sting in my thigh caught my attention, and I reached down to grab the tufted dart sticking out of my skin.

"Ah, fudge nuggets, not again." I slumped over.

CHAPTER 15

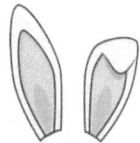

GOING from catching his breath after an intense orgasm to waking in a puddle of his own drool proved jarring. Especially since Claire was no longer straddling his body or touching him in any way, shape, or form.

The stone floor was gone, replaced by something smoother, and there was a slight vibration along with the hum of an engine.

I'm being moved.

Shit.

Derek lifted his head and noticed he currently resided in a cage, one of many stacked inside the transport truck, and not a big cage he might add. He couldn't even stand upright in it. It was made of metal bars welded into a rectangle that was taller than it was wide. The door was chained shut and held closed by a thick padlock.

Not exactly the most promising situation. The good, if disturbing, news, though?

He wasn't alone. More cages surrounded him—left, right, and across—plus he was in a second row. His metal pen sat perched on top of another, the occupant below him not visible due to a plastic tray lining the bottom. He fingered the smooth surface.

Over the rumble of the truck's engine, he heard a rough voice say, "It's in case you make a mess."

Looking across the aisle between his cage and the next, Derek saw a man...if someone covered in hair, hunched with his knees up to his chin, sporting apish features could be called a man.

"Before you ask, yes, I am Sasquatch. No, my name's not Harry, and I don't know the Hendersons."

"Well shoot, there goes our whole conversation," Derek couldn't help but drawl. The situation wasn't humorous, but that didn't mean he had to turn to doom and gloom. "And I am a werewolf who stupidly went poking around a secret lab and got caught. Guess I'll be a contender for the Darwin Awards. Name's Derek by the way."

"Ethan," replied the other male. "Everyone told me to not leave the valley. Humans are dangerous they said. Guess I should have listened." His lips turned down.

"Do you know where we are going?" Derek

asked, glancing around, doing more than a cursory inspection this time.

The cages to his left and right each held bodies, the occupants sleeping, their faces slack, eyes closed. Those that didn't rest crouched and rocked. Except for the thing in the large tank at the very back of the trailer. It floated. A man-like upper body replete with long, flowing beard and white hair. Below the waist? Pure tail. The scales dull and dark.

I think I just found Neptune.

Which meant... He glanced around until he saw a woman with a gag in her mouth. She sat with her head leaning on the bars. Had to be Bella the siren. But what of Claire? He didn't see her in any of the top layer of cages. Nor the lower ones that he could see.

Gripping the bars, he realized he could barely get his hand out, which meant no breaking the lock. He couldn't reach it. He pressed his face to the bars and craned to see. "Enny? You there, Enny?"

"Yes, I'm here. Where else would I be since they stuffed me in a cage and *stole* my stash of chocolate," she exclaimed.

He wasn't surprised by the fact she sounded more bothered by the theft. "I might have a protein bar tucked in my pocket."

"Is this an invitation to grope?"

He knelt since it appeared she was below him. "You don't need an invite," he said in a low voice.

Someone gagged.

He didn't care. Hearing her voice relieved his mind. They were both alive, which meant they just had to escape.

"I will definitely take you up on that offer once things settle down," Claire remarked.

An odd thing to say. "Are you hurt?"

"No. But I am craving a chocolate bar. Or some carrot cake, extra cream cheese icing. My skin's also getting itchy, which means the moon is about to rise."

"You can feel that?" He usually needed direct moonlight to sense anything.

"It's almost here, and I don't think it will be pretty."

With her ominous tone, he had to wonder what she was talking about, and then it hit him. Was she talking about her period? "Are you bleeding?" he whispered. Did she worry about setting off some of the people in cages? Although, people might be generous. A few were much more messed up than Ethan and Neptune. He spotted a few hybrids that probably had a scientific helping hand.

"There will be blood. I'm sure they thought the cage would be enough. But then again, they probably didn't know. They should have asked me. I haven't yet seen a place that can hold me."

"What are you talking about?"

"The full moon, Big. I probably should have

mentioned it before. I tend to go a little crazy once a month."

"Are you talking about PMS?"

"Worse than that."

"You're not making any sense." Had someone drugged Claire?

"Don't you worry, Big. It will soon become clear. I hope you'll respect me in the morning." She giggled. "Actually, it might be better if you didn't. We'll have more fun that way."

"You do realize we're prisoners." He wasn't sure if she'd spotted the obvious.

"Not for much longer," she sang. "I'd say, within the next half-hour, you'll be free. Everyone will be."

"Are you referring to the Vikings you called in? They won't find us. We're being moved."

"We won't make our final destination. We are getting out of here, Big. As for the cavalry, they'll find us. Lana always knows how to locate me."

"Lana is in bed at home."

"Of course she is, silly." He heard a giggle. "She'll send Jory. Which is probably better. He only decimates his enemies. With Lana, you gotta be careful because she's a killer singer." He heard a rustle.

"What are you doing?"

"Stripping."

"Um, why?" Curiosity did much to curb his jealousy.

"Because I might need something to wear after I shift."

"Why on earth would you shift?" How was being a bunny the best choice in this situation?

"I won't have a choice. The moon thing and all."

"We're in a sealed trailer."

"Won't matter."

"What do you mean won't matter? Don't you have control over your shifting?" Because most learned how to keep the change from happening in their teens.

"My bunny is special."

"I'm going to try and get out of my cage." Even metal bars could have a weakness. He gripped the cool rods and pulled. Pushed. Heaved his body against them, until Ethan across from him sighed.

"They're titanium."

"I just." Grunt. "Need." Grrr. "One." Ugh. "Weak spot."

"And do what if you escape?" Ethan reached out and grabbed the bars with long and thick fingers that barely made it through the gap. "The cages aren't the real problems." The Sasquatch barely seemed to strain as he yanked them apart. He did it with all the bars until he had a large hole. Ethan wiggled out and stood in the aisle, tall enough to look inside Derek's cage.

"Damn, dude, those are some serious guns." Derek admired the strength in the other guy.

Ethan misunderstood. "I have no weapon."

"I was talking about your arms. Your strength. Mind helping a guy out?" He pointed to his bars. "Let's blow this joint."

"How do you plan to escape?" asked Ethan. "This truck is part of a convoy. Trucks ahead and behind us filled with armed men. If it's like previous times, they'll have a helicopter overhead sweeping our path. More than likely armed with heat sensors and machine guns."

Hardcore shit. However, remaining a prisoner wasn't an option. "It's a chance I'm willing to take."

"You'll fail."

"Won't know unless I try, so why not help me out of this cage?"

"If you insist." Derek stood back and waited for Ethan to heave the bars apart. Instead he crushed the lock overhead holding the door shut. The cage swung open, and Derek leapt out, landing on his feet and wobbling.

"Freedom!" Claire shouted.

A few more voices rose asking for the same chance, including Claire, who said, "You are da bomb, Ethan honey. You should seriously try entering some arm wrestling contest. And is it me or are your feet huge?"

"Claire," Derek groaned, closing his eyes for a second. He faced Ethan. "Don't listen to her. She is obviously under some kind of drug-induced delusion that her rabbit will save the day."

"Because it will," she exclaimed.

A scowl pulled Ethan's lips. "Trying to leave is madness. Take it from someone who's tried before."

"You want to just give up?" The very thought was repugnant to Derek. "We can't let them win. This is our best chance to escape, here and now, while we're in transit because once they shove us in another mountain—"

"The experiments start anew," Ethan interrupted. "As someone in their custody for almost twenty years, I am well aware of what they do."

The length of Ethan's stay proved sobering, but Derek couldn't stop now. He wasn't about to become a prisoner for life. "You want to endure twenty more?"

Ethan gave him a hard stare. "Do you have a plan?"

"Depends. How good are you at ripping off arms and using them as weapons?" Judging by Ethan's wide eyes, nope.

"I can do it!" Claire insisted.

"Where are you, Enny?"

"Right behind you, admiring your ass." He whirled and caught her big smile and wave. She wore the T-shirt and panties of before.

"Mind giving me a hand?" Derek pointed, and Ethan grasped the lock. It cracked open.

The truck slowed down.

"Shit. They must have cameras watching." Derek glanced up and down the aisle of cages. Some with faces peering curiously. No weapons in sight. "Ethan, open as many cages as you can. Go after the ones who are awake first. They can help."

"Or you can all sit down and let me handle this." Claire placed a hand on Derek's chest. "It will be all right. I can do this. I feel the panic attack coming on now, which means it won't be long."

She wasn't the only one panicking. His heart raced, too, as he realized what he'd have to do. "Listen, Enny. We won't have much time when that door opens. Soon as it does, I'm going to distract any guards waiting outside. Once I do, I want you and Ethan and anyone who can run to take off in opposing directions.

"How are you planning to distract them?" she asked with a furrowed brow.

"You let me worry about that." Because he already knew she wouldn't like his plan.

The back of the trailer clanked and rattled as someone unlocked the door.

"You won't need to do a thing, Big. The moon's almost here," she murmured, staring overhead. "I just need a minute."

The doors at the back of the van creaked as they began to swing open. "We don't have a minute." He turned to her and pressed his mouth against hers. A hard embrace that had to say everything he'd never had a chance to say before. "I love you, Claire Mahoney."

Then, before he could change his mind, he ran for the doors, tearing at his clothes, letting his wolf burst free with a howl that roused the others in the cages.

He didn't look back. Couldn't afford to stumble.

The guns aimed inside the open door—hopefully with tranquilizers, but probably bullets too—didn't stop his charge as he hit the ground with four feet. An ululating battle cry emerged from his muzzle as he leaped. The first few gunshots went off and missed. He slammed into the first mercenary he saw and might have hesitated at the human form pinned under him until he saw the eyes, slitted and a malevolent yellow.

Not human.

He grabbed it by the throat and bit down hard. Managed to kill the hybrid before turning to another. Before he could pounce again, *crack*!

The bullet hit him in the shoulder. The second in the leg.

He couldn't stop the whimper at the sudden shock and pain. He slumped, muzzle hitting the ground.

The barrel of a gun was placed between his eyes.

"Don't you dare hurt him," Claire screamed as he snarled.

He didn't want to die, but his leg wouldn't support his wolf. So he changed back, hoping it would startle the gunman enough he wouldn't shoot.

It worked; the barrel pulled back as he writhed on the ground in agony. The pain of the change rolling into that of his wounds. But the agony of failure hurt more.

Sorry, Enny. Derek rolled onto his back hoping for one last look at her and thus saw the massive furry body that leapt from the truck.

White-furred. Long-eared. With enormous saber teeth and claws.

"Claire?" he mumbled before passing out.

CHAPTER 16

A CAVALRY INTERMISSION

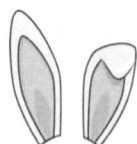

THERE WAS JOSTLING on the helicopter, the ragtag group of Vikings unused to actually having to fly anywhere. Usually they could simply use a portal to get places, but the Rockies were an exception.

After a few ales, Sven got scientific and explained it as a glitch in the force. In other words, the portal magic was disrupted by something radiating from the mountains. He theorized it had some kind of super-metal inside them. Even had a fancy word for it that the Vikings all mocked.

In a nutshell it meant esoteric stuff like portals were out. Even scrying didn't work.

The lack meant using human methods to travel. Such as helicopters, which were made for smaller people. Vikings tended to be a strapping bunch.

The pilot kept cursing. "Stop your fucking moving around or I'll set you down right here, right now."

"Calm yourself," Jory said to the man. "We are almost there." He kept an eye on the screen displaying a map and a blinking red dot.

"I can see the lights of the convoy," Neil announced. "It doesn't appear to be moving."

"Odd place to stop," Jory remarked. By all indications the area was bereft of civilization. "Could they have had a mechanical failure?

The earpiece in his ear crackled, the signal weak. "What's this about the convoy? Have you found her?" Lana asked, following the excursion from a tub at home.

"Not yet. I'm going in for a closer look." Jory spoke knowing his tiny microphone, part of his earpiece, would pick up the words and relay it. "V Squadron, are you ladies keeping pace?"

A female voice replied with a dry, "We've already been ahead and back. Your mechanical wings are slow." The Valkyries did so like to tease about their abilities.

Jory never rose to the bait. As a half-blood—half god, half Valkyrie—it meant that when he dove out of the helicopter, shouting, "Bombs away," wings burst from his back. Big, dark ones that caught the air and filled him with weightless elation. He didn't bask for long, as a strapping body plummeted past him.

"Everyone in the V Squadron, Viking up," he shouted.

More bodies jumped from the helicopter; Neil,

Sven, and others who volunteered. While Anya grabbed hold of Neil, Jory dove at his target, Ralph, who'd leaped first once again. He swooped in and grabbed the man under the arms, slowing his descent with heavy pulls of his wings.

"You been sneaking loaves of bread again?" Jory asked.

"You calling me fat?" snarled Ralph.

"Yes," Jory chuckled. "But that cushion will come in handy for the landing. I hear a bird incoming." Indeed, the whir of another bird in the sky approached. He released his comrade, throwing him at a tall tree. As he swept past in an arc, he saw Ralph grab a branch and swing.

Then Jory was off, wings flapping hard as he headed upwards and over to where the whirring sound of another helicopter drew his eye.

Rat-tat-tat. Gunfire erupted as the enemy on board noticed their incoming dilemma.

Bullets didn't stop Valkyries. With shouts of glee, three came swooping in, eyes alight with battle lust, claws extended.

Jory, on the other hand, pulled a sword. Never got a chance to use it.

V Squadron took down the bird, jamming a soldier in its blades, mangling it. The helicopter listed, almost righted itself, then Anya plastered herself on the windshield and began pummeling it.

Since they didn't need his help, Jory went after the convoy on the ground.

"Vikings, sound off." A chorus of names sang in his headset, and he noted them all accounted for except for Peter. "Did anyone see Peter?"

"Here. Fuck. My balls. Damn. Bitch crushed my manhood."

It took but a moment for Jory to finally spot Peter, in the vee of a tree, hugging the bole of it. Moaning.

"Guess you'll be buying the drinks," Jory taunted as he hit the ground running. The one with the least kills paid because it was damned embarrassing.

With his feet planted on terra firma, Jory oriented himself. An aerial glimpse had shown four ground vehicles, dark SUVs with headlights gleaming. One truck appeared to have a light broken and its hood dented. There was also lots of broken glass as if a battle had already occurred.

"What's happening?" Lana asked. "What can you see?"

"Looks like something already hit the convoy." And not long ago by the looks of it. The engines still ticked as they cooled. The blood was fresh and damp, not yet begun to dry.

"I didn't expect it to hit so soon. I thought the time change would delay it," Lana muttered. "She must have panicked."

"You can't mean..." Jory hesitated as he looked around, noticing the mangled bodies on the ground, all wearing uniforms. Nah. Not sweet, innocent Claire. He knew the woman fairly well by now. She couldn't stand to even kill a fly.

The back of the truck loomed open; however, the interior didn't appear empty. Jory approached and saw faces peering out. Frightened faces.

Before he could question them on what had happened, snarls erupted from the woods and wolves poured out. Larger than normal wolves, their leader a big, grizzled fellow who paused a few paces from Jory and snarled.

So Jory snarled back. The wolf, though, had no interest in Jory. It darted to the side and headed for a body on the ground.

The first one he'd seen not in a uniform and, given the nudity, probably a shapeshifter.

As the wolf let out a baying howl, Jory walked the scene and spoke quietly to his wife.

"Um, Lana, there's an awful lot of damage here. I think something escaped that truck. Something big and mean." Impressive enough he wanted to buy whatever it was a beer.

"I don't know if I'd call it big and mean. Unless you touch her chocolate."

"Hold on, you're not saying... Claire did this?" The bodies. The door ripped from its frame and used to smash another soldier to a pulp.

"She tends to go a little wild when she panics."

"You don't say." Now he wanted to buy her two beers and a chocolate sundae. Because damn. Claire was a bunny berserker.

CHAPTER 17

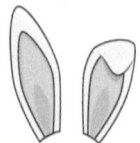

I awoke naked, as usual. Covered in blood. Again, kind of the norm. What was kind of weird was having Jory leaning over me but having Lana's voice haranguing.

"...throw some clothes on her. Don't you dare be peeking at my best friend's goodies, or I will eat your eyeballs."

"She will," I noted. "With lemon squeezed on top."

"Probably with a side of pickles." Jory grinned. He shook out his hands, and fabric draped over me.

I clung to it, tucking it around, before sitting up.

"Is she okay? Tell me if she's hurt." The voice emerged from an earpiece dangling around Jory's neck.

"How are you?" Jory rumbled.

"Fine. Where am I?" Last time I woke up, I was in a transport truck locked in a cage.

"We're in the woods."

"Duh." I knew that. "What happened? Where's Derek?" Because I seemed to remember Derek telling me he loved me before diving out of the truck and getting shot. Idiot. He just couldn't wait.

"By the looks of it, you saved the day."

"Did I?" I preferred not to dig too deep because, last thing I truly recalled, my skin tingled. My bunny quivered. My panic was rising, and then Derek went down. Shot in front of my eyes! "I told him to hold on and let me handle it. I knew my inner ninja bunny wouldn't let me down."

"Ninja?"

I sighed. "Is this where you agree with Lana and say none of my moves are ninja-ish?"

"Alas, I arrived too late to enjoy the battle. However, I did see the aftermath." Jory held out a bottle of water, which I grabbed and chugged greedily. "Given the destruction wrought on thine enemies, I would say Claire the Berserker would be apt."

"The berserker, hunh? I like that." I grinned. "Wait until I tell Derek."

The expression on Jory's face went blank, setting off my uh-oh meter.

"What is it? What happened to Derek?" I grabbed Jory by the lapels and shook him, "Tell me!" Even as Lana shrieked, "Your pet wolf is fine. Don't kill the father of my unborn child."

Realizing I held Jory off the ground—only an inch given I was short, but still, manhandling him—I set him down and composed myself. "Tell me what you know. I remember him getting shot, but it was only two bullets. He should have been fine."

"Two?" Jory snorted. "Last I saw, the showoff sported at least eight. According to the survivors, he rose and continued to fight. Quite the scrapper apparently. When he saw some soldiers band together, about to shoot your ferocious beast, he threw himself in front of the bullets."

I closed my eyes and counted to ten before I exploded. "Oh my God, that idiot. How can a man being so stupid and also be the most sexiest awesome thing ever?" I paused, opened one eye, and said, "He did survive, right?"

"Yes. He is expected to make a full recovery."

"Sweet!" I fist-pumped. Someone was so getting icing licked off his body the moment I saw him. "Take me to him."

"Um, I can't."

"Why not?"

"Lana said not to."

"What?" I glared at the earpiece around his neck and addressed it. "You can't keep me from seeing Derek."

The man had stopped a bullet for me. Told me he loved me. I needed to see him. Now.

Lana's reply froze me. "His family showed up at

the scene of the attack and took him back to your old hometown before Jory could find you."

Eep.

He was gone.

I'd lost him.

Because there was no way I could follow. No way.

But...

I love him.

Did I love him enough to face my family? The panic rose. My skin tingled. Lana yelled, "Don't let her freak out. If you see her nose twitching, run."

Running wouldn't work. I knew that for a fact. I'd run for ten years and still couldn't escape my past. The question was, had the time come to face it?

CHAPTER 18

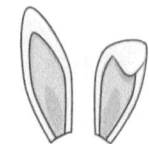

Claire waltzed in with a bounce to her blonde hair, and Derek froze, halfway dressed, one leg in his jeans, the other still out. He'd woken up not long ago and, when he found out Claire wasn't with him, informed his family he had to leave.

"Leave? You're still leaking blood!" his mother shrieked.

"Showoff," muttered his brother.

They didn't understand. He had to find her.

Only, there she was. In the vibrant flesh, looking gorgeous despite the T-shirt that claimed, "I kissed a Sasquatch." She better not have. He'd hate to kill Ethan.

"You came." He wondered if he hallucinated.

"Of course I did. I had to see you." She chewed her lower lip. "Are you okay?"

"I am now. I'm so happy you came." He opened his arms, and she threw herself at him.

Being a man, he didn't wince even when she slammed into a few wounds. Having her close by made him feel a million times better.

Until she reared back and slugged him in the arm, right atop a bandage. "You idiot."

"What the hell?"

"You stood in front of bullets for me."

"And?"

"That is the stupidest thing you could have done." She burst into tears. "That is the most beautiful thing anyone has ever done for me."

He enveloped her in his arms. "I meant what I said."

"You really love me?" she sniffled. She raised her head, lashes wet.

"Have ever since we were kids." He stroked her hair back from her face. "Now it's my turn to ask. Are you all right? No one knew what happened to you after the battle." He'd passed out from the second round of gunshot wounds and only woken in spurts as he was carried to safety. When he finally did regain consciousness, his brothers treated him to a rendition of the battle relayed to them by the survivors that spoke of a gigantic bunny with razor-sharp claws and giant ears rampaging and saving the day.

Claire. Apparently, she went really ballistic after he was shot enough to keep him down on the ground. His brother showed him footage of the aftermath with the broken cars and bodies. She'd pulverized the enemy.

"I told you we'd escape." She beamed, but there was a hint of hesitation in it.

He didn't let her pull away. "You were amazing."

"Was I?"

"How could you think otherwise? You won the day, Enny."

"I killed people."

"Bad people. I was doing the same. And you should know, I was going to come find you. You just didn't let me get my pants on first." Those pants were actually on the floor.

"I like you better out of them," she cutely admitted.

He lifted her chin. "It means a lot to me that you came."

"I wasn't sure if I should, after what happened." Her head ducked, and it took him a moment to realize why.

"Hold on a second. Are you embarrassed?"

She shrugged. "My bunny isn't exactly normal, as you saw."

"Your bunny kicks ass," he exclaimed.

"Only when it goes into monster mode."

"Why would you call it that?"

"It's a killing machine."

"It's a warrior. Like you."

"Me?" She glanced at him.

"Yes, you. I hear that, because of you, all the people they had locked up were freed." Which some might have found emasculating; however, Derek saw it a positive thing they'd all survived and those imprisoned found freedom again. "You did that. You and your special awesome bunny."

"I guess." She shrugged. "Lana finally got to meet her real mom and dad. Jory said she squealed so loud all the smoke alarms went off in the building and the firemen were called."

"That reunion wouldn't have happened without you."

"Guess I was a hero." Her smile returned.

"Totally."

"Does this mean for Halloween we both get to wear tights and be Superman?"

"I don't do tights."

"How about a loin cloth? You'd make an epic Conan."

"How about we worry about that next year. First, there's something you need to do. Something to make this day just perfect." He winked.

She sighed. "Do I have to?" She fidgeted with his hair and nuzzled his neck.

"Only if you're in the mood," he replied, cupping her ass.

"I'll do it. But after, you'd better be prepared to give me the best sex of my life."

Hold on. That was what he planned, except she

dropped a kiss on his lips and turned around to walk out the door.

"Where are you going?" he asked.

"Where do you think, silly? To face my parents."

CHAPTER 19

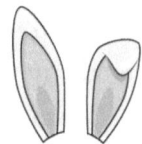

Hardest thing ever. I walked a road I knew and yet, at the same time, didn't. When had the trees in the front yard gotten so big? The lilac so tall?

I loved the red they'd painted the front door. The frilly curtains in the front window were a change from the wooden blinds that were rarely shut. The vehicle in the driveway wasn't the same pickup truck my dad owned a decade ago, but it was still a big Dodge Ram, king cab, the paint job a deep blue. My dad used to keep a bag of licorice in the glovebox for us to share when I went on rides with him into the big city for a Costco run. I wonder if he stopped doing that when I left.

I wondered a lot of things about my family. Most of all, what would they say when they saw me at the door?

My pulse raced. Pitter-patter. I was terrified. More scared than when I was caught by the demon.

More frightened than the time I stole Lana's donut when she was PMS-ing.

However, I'd learned one crucial thing since I'd left home. Fear was normal. It was how you handled the fear that counted. Learning how to cope had made me strong.

Strong enough to do this.

It took effort and deep breaths to walk up those steps. My inner bunny was ready to turn tail and run. But I wouldn't let fear chase me away again.

Before I could knock, the door was flung open and my mother stared at me. I froze in place, not even my nose twitched. My heart, though, it thumped, fast enough I wondered if I was having a heart attack. The urge to flee beat fast as a drum inside me.

I took a step forward instead. "Hey, Mom."

My mother had aged in the last decade. Lines marked the corners of her eyes and forehead. Her hair held a hint of gray. She'd been over forty when I left and now was pushing fifty-five.

That said, she looked damned good even if her lips trembled and her eyes glistened with tears.

"Claire? Is that really you?" Spoken in a quavering voice.

I found my throat tight. Too tight to speak so I nodded.

"Oh, baby girl." Her arms came around me in a hug I'd not realized I'd missed until that moment.

Okay, so maybe I had missed it. I'd just shoved it down far enough inside that I made myself believe I didn't need it.

But I did. I needed my mommy and missed her. I let it all out sobbing against her shoulder. Sobbed and snotted and apologized while she hugged me. And we couldn't have been there more than two minutes before I heard the sound of pounding feet. I didn't even have time to turn. I was lifted in the air and smothered by a chest.

I didn't mind the rib-crushing hug my dad gave me, and I didn't have to question how he knew I was home. His bond with my mom was strong, enough that they shared feelings sometimes.

Could he feel my shame that I'd ever believed they didn't love me enough to handle the fact I was different? Could I ever apologize enough for being a teenager who, in her pompous self-centeredness, thought it was better to leave the people who loved her most?

"I'm sorry," I managed to mumble in a teary voice.

"Princess." My dad sighed my nickname. "Thank the moon lord you're home."

"Actually, you should thank Derek. He's the one who guilted me into coming." It seemed important to give him credit. No more lies.

Daddy set me down, and my mother wrapped

her arm around my waist. "Come inside, baby girl. I'll make you something to eat."

The drool just about hit the ground at the mention. Mom was an epic cook. She could literally whip together anything with the meanest of ingredients. Stuck in the woods with pine tree and moss and not much else? She'd hunt down the edible leaves, snare a wild turkey, stuff it and roast it over an open fire.

Don't believe it? I'd eaten it. And the raspberry coulee she made for dessert dribbled over a fresh honeycomb? My tummy rumbled.

Entering my home was the same and yet so different. Some of the furniture had changed, like the old comfy couch was now a bigger, plusher version. The television in its wooden box swapped for a massive flat screen. But the clock on the wall was still the one grandpa had made my mom. The pictures on the mantel, my family. Me, Mom, Dad... Smiling back in a time before my world changed.

I picked up one of my dad swinging me in the air.

He stood behind me. "When you were little, you always trusted me to never let you fall."

"Because I knew you wouldn't."

"I wish you'd remembered that when you got scared."

I ducked my head, and tears threatened. He hugged me again. "Don't cry. I didn't mean to say it as punishment. I'm the one who's sorry. I should have worked harder to make you feel accepted and loved."

"I thought you hated me for being different."

"Never," my mother exclaimed, joining the family hug. "We were worried, and we should have spent more time talking to you than to doctors."

"The important thing is you're home now," my dad stated.

And it was still my home.

My room appeared absolutely the same. Down to the makeup in the vanity. Dried out and useless now, but another indication of how much my family missed me. Which was why when dinner ended, and we'd spent hours catching up, I agreed to stay the night. My mother had a hard time seeing me off to bed.

She kept touching me. Afraid I'd disappear.

I wouldn't. I might not be able to change the past, but I could do something about the future.

However, speaking of future, there was someone else I had to see. I thought about going back downstairs and using the front door like an adult, but...I grinned as I threw up the sash to my window and sat on the sill.

I stopped before swinging my legs out. I hopped back into my room, found a pad of paper and a stub of a pencil in my nightstand, and left a note on my bed.

Gone to bother Derek. I will be back in a bit. Love Claire.

Just in case they checked on me, I didn't want them thinking I'd ditched them again.

I exited the window and balanced on the slim porch, making my way over to the trellis. It was a little trickier to climb than I remembered. I'd not kept in practice living in the city. I made it to the ground in one piece and began walking across the back lawn that edged the woods. Derek was staying with his folks, and that was only a few streets over, so imagine my surprise when I heard a whistle.

He stepped out from behind a tree and cocked a brow. "Going somewhere, Enny?"

"To see you, as a matter of fact."

"What a coincidence. I was doing the same." He walked toward me. "How did it go with your parents?"

"Good. Lots of crying." I grimaced. "Lots of chocolate cake." I rubbed my belly and smiled. "Thank you."

"For what?"

"For helping me realize I could come back home."

"I think deep down you always knew you could."

"I wish I'd reminded myself sooner." My nose wrinkled. "Wanna come back to my room?"

"And end up killed by your father for deflowering his daughter? Uh, no," he said with a wry grin.

"Were you planning some debauchery, Big? Because I would totally be up for that."

"Claire Mahoney, are you trying to seduce me?"

"Who says I'm trying. I *am* seducing you." I stepped close enough to grab him around the hips and pulled him close. A seductive smile teased my lips. "Kiss me."

"I want to do more than kiss."

"Then take me. Claim me." I leaned up on tiptoe. "I love you, too."

His arms crushed me at that point, and it didn't matter we had no bed. I was going to have him.

Right here. Right now.

Our lips melded together in a searing kiss. I melted against him, loving the tight wrap of his arms. The only way this hug could be improved was if we wore fewer clothes.

I shoved away from him and stripped off my nightie, leaving on only my underpants. I then insisted he take off his shirt. Running my hands over the toned smoothness of his body delighted me. Except for the bullet holes. Red, puckered wounds on his skin.

I kissed each of them, the unmistakable symbol of his love for me.

"You missed one," he said.

"Hold on a second." I undid his pants and pushed his jeans down around his ankles. Another mark on his thigh earned a kiss. As for his shaft...

I pressed my mouth to it and blew hotly. He groaned and reached down to yank me up. "Don't you dare start."

"Or what?" I asked, feathering kisses on his jaw. "Because it's my turn." Between one heartbeat and the next, he had me pressed up against a tree, and he dropped to his knees, raising the hem of my short nightgown. Each inch he lifted had an accompanying kiss on my thigh. Left leg. Right. He moved up, and I leaned against the rough bark, reached behind to grasp it to hold myself steady. When he reached my panties, he mouthed me through the fabric. A poor scrap of silk that didn't stand a chance when he ripped it.

Not that I minded. Let him lick me.

Except he didn't lick. He instead ran his fingers over my wet lips and then flicked my clit. My hips arched right into his face.

His mouth was there to catch me, his tongue to tease me further. He lapped at me until I moaned and squirmed.

Only then did he rise and spin me around, warning me with a soft growl to, "Brace yourself."

I grabbed hold of that tree and pushed out my bottom. I throbbed for his touch. Ached for him to fill me. He flipped my nightgown up over my butt and parted my thighs by inserting his foot between mine. He guided his rigid shaft between my cheeks, rubbing it against my damp cleft, teasing it over my swollen button.

I wiggled and tossed him a coy look. "Do I have to get on my knees again to get some action?"

In reply, he pushed himself between my nether lips. Sank himself deep inside me, making me feel whole.

But that was only the beginning. He began to thrust, in and out of me, working up a rhythm that brought short pants and dug my nails into the bark.

He slammed into me, and I welcomed the thickness of him. Craved it. I could feel the pleasure building inside me. The satisfying sound of slapping flesh joined by our dual moans.

Reaching that blissful edge, I gasped. "Bite me. Mark me."

"Are you sure?" he murmured as he leaned forward along the curve of my spine.

"I don't want to ever lose you." Not again. I'd finally found what I'd been missing in my life, and I wasn't about to ever let it go.

His hips slowed their pounding to grind against me as he nuzzled my shoulder. He sucked on the skin while reaching for my breasts. Cupping them. Kneading them. Rolling my nipples into hard points.

I gasped for air by that point, at that cusp where pleasure made me whimper as if in pain. I ached. I needed.

He bit me and unleashed my climax. It rippled

through my body. Caused my channel to flex and squeeze the length of him. Milking him.

I felt more than heard his rumble as he came, his teeth still buried in skin, creating a connection between us that only death would part.

Our heaving and moaning stilled. Our bodies cooled. I giggled.

"What's so funny?" he asked.

"Do you realize we've yet to make it to a bed?"

He pulled out of me, and I turned around to face him. "And that's a bad thing because?" he asked with an arched brow.

"I love you." The words burst from me, and I threw my arms around his neck. When he kissed me, I bit him.

He didn't complain, although he did yelp. "Did you have to tear off half my lip?"

"It's just a flesh wound. Don't tell me you're afraid of my nasty big pointy teeth?"

"Please tell me you meant to half-ass quote Monty Python." He sounded so hopeful.

"Blessed are the cheesemakers."

For some reason this made him insanely happy. He lifted me off the ground and whirled me around.

I only wished I could bring him home, but Derek was right. My daddy might just kill him if he found Derek in my bed. But I'd see him first thing in the morning.

Bunny Misfit

He saw me to my trellis, watched me climb in. I blew him a kiss before shutting the window.

I sighed happily.

So this was love. I rather liked it. Lucky me I'd get to enjoy it every day as the throb in my shoulder reminded me I'd just been mated.

I wanted to giggle and shout it to the world. I should be quiet lest my parents hear me.

Speaking of hearing... A hum of voices appeared to be coming from downstairs.

I crept to the edge of the hall and listened. Bad, I know. However, it wasn't just kitties that were curious.

The murmur proved indistinct. So I moved closer and finally began to make out phrases.

"...like I already told you, she's not here," my dad said.

"Impossible. The tracking device shows her nearby. You can't hide her forever." My eyes widened as I recognized the voice despite having only heard it once.

Dr. Creepy. How dare he disturb my parents.

I was ready to charge into that room and rip him to shreds when a noise from behind stopped me. My nose wrinkled at the lack of smell a moment before the needle slipped into my skin and I murmured, "Oh Fudgsicle. Not again."

CHAPTER 20

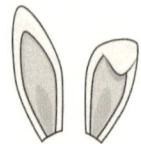

Derek meant to go home. He even made it to the edge of the woods before he turned around.

Something is wrong. Claire was in danger. He couldn't have said how he knew; he just felt it.

He began walking back to Claire's house. A wisp of smoke tickled his nose. He broke into a jog as he saw an orange glow coming from behind some curtains.

Fire! Every animal's most base fear.

"Claire!" He yelled her name, even as he knew she couldn't answer. He raced around the side of the house to the front, the slam of car doors drawing him.

A man in spectacles turned to gape at him, and Derek instantly hated him. He smelled wrong. Of hospitals and blood. It didn't help the man's cause that he yelled, "Don't come near me or I'll shoot."

Derek snarled, "Where is Claire, asshole?"

The fellow chose to turn his back and put his hand on the passenger door.

Like hell was he escaping. Bigger teeth pushed from Derek's gums and filled his mouth while claws tipped his fingers, but he kept his man shape as he plowed into the guy with glasses. They hit the ground hard, the fellow squeaking. The man himself wasn't a threat, he whimpered under Derek's weight, but there was no mercy in him, not once he caught a whiff of his mate.

He lowered his face to the man's shirt, but the scent wasn't coming from him. Derek looked at the car.

Before he could wrench at a door, it swung open and smacked him. He reeled back and snapped.

"You." A word growled as Derek glared at the man stepping out of the car.

"Yes me, puppy chow."

"I thought you were dead." Derek cracked his knuckles. "Guess I should rectify that."

"You wanna go, let's go, then." Toby tore off his sunglasses, and his flesh bulked, his body thickening and ripping the seams of his shirt.

Rather than wait to see what monstrous hybrid he would become, Derek leaped.

Toby dodged, his body still changing. Derek swung around, his hybrid shape hard to hold but powerful, given Toby was turning into some type of lizard man.

Derek dove at him again, grabbing the other guy by the arms, grappling with him. His jaw opened wide, and they struggled, Derek snapping his teeth.

The fellow on the ground proved helpful finally as he tried to crawl away and instead tripped Toby. They went down in a heap, and Derek finally managed to clasp the scaled neck. He chomped down and yet very little crunched.

Derek didn't let that stop him from shaking his head. Toby braced his arms under his body and shoved, flinging him away. Fuck the hybrid shape. Derek shifted even before he hit the ground. He wanted the skill of his wolf for this battle.

Rising to his paws, he dove again, this time going for the ankles, dodging Toby's shortened arms. He wrapped his muzzle around a limb and earned a satisfying crunch as flesh split and bone cracked.

Toby yelled and tried to remain standing on one leg. That plan failed when Derek switched ankles. Once the guy hit the ground, it was over quickly.

Derek shook the blood from his muzzle and eyed the car. The man in the glasses had recovered and sat behind the wheel cursing as the engine revved but the car didn't move. "Who the hell rents a standard transmission?"

Shifting back to his man shape, Derek reached in and yanked out the keys.

"You're not going anywhere, little man. Where's Claire?"

"Here." She popped up from the back looking tousled and bleary eyed. "What happened?"

"You were being kidnapped again."

"Again!" she squeaked. "Seriously. What part of 'get lost' did you not get, Dr. Creepy? Once I stop seeing three of you, I am going to rip your head off and shove it up your hiney."

For his part, the scientist didn't look perturbed. "You won't kill me."

"I'm pretty sure I will, and if I don't, Derek or my daddy will. Research shows once an evil scientist always an evil scientist. Only one thing to do." She ran a finger over her neck and made an odd squicking noise.

"How did you know where she was?" Derek asked, hauling the man out of the car and holding him aloft.

"Tracking device. All the subjects have one. Even you." The doctor smirked.

Derek slapped it off and shook him again. "Where is it? How do we get it out?"

"You hit me!" Dr. Creepy squealed. "You aren't supposed to hit a man with glasses."

"I don't see a man." He looked to Claire. "Do you see a man?"

"Nope. Just a yellow-bellied coward. And don't worry about the tracking chips. I have a friend who can remove them."

"Why did you come here?" Derek asked. "Surely

you didn't think you and your pet project could waltz in here and take her?" Never mind the fact it almost worked.

"I had to once I realized what you had become. I never imagined it worked."

"What worked?" Claire asked.

"Did your parents never tell you?" the doctor taunted. "They had fertility issues. They required aid getting pregnant, and they came to me. Imagine my surprise when I realized how different their DNA was."

"Oh dear," Claire murmured as she emerged from the car.

But Derek was the one to say it aloud. "You mean you're the reason Claire—"

"Transforms into a killing machine. Yes! Once I realized how special your parents were, I modified their fertility treatment, adding some tweaks."

It didn't take much to follow what the doctor did. What better gene to mix in than one for bunnies because everyone always joked about how well they multiplied.

Most people would be horrified to find out they were the result of a mad science experiment. Claire, though...she smiled. "I'm a real misfit, just like my besties. But I think it's time your projects came to an end."

She reached for the doctor, and he cried out. "No. If you kill me, you'll never find the rest."

"Wrong. If I kill you, I will find the rest. Because now we're looking."

He never would know if Claire would have killed the wimp in cold blood because the man suddenly gasped, his lips turned blue, and he keeled over.

Heart attack.

The door to the house was wrenched open by a seething, half-shifted alpha. "Princess." The guttural word was barely discernible.

"I'm okay, Da—" As if she got to finish that sentence. She got squished in a hug that swept her off her feet.

"Awooo!"

The mournful howl came from Claire's mom, who stood looking disheveled in her robe, staring at her smoking house. There was no saving it.

That night, even though only her parents' house burned to the ground, everyone in the pack lost their home. Despite Dr. Creepy having died of heart failure, a decision was made to scatter rather than risk exposing the pack.

As discussions occurred about where to move, Claire couldn't stop exclaiming it was all her fault and felt horrible until she realized something. "You can all come live with me."

Except even that plan fell through after Jory caught someone spying on the apartment. Which was why everyone relocated to Quebec.

Mostly because, after much deliberation, Claire declared that, despite its lack of chocolate factories, the French province in Canada had delectable maple candy treats and poutine.

Not everyone from the pack moved with them. Some chose to join other shifter packs. Others decided to try the lone wolf route.

As for Derek and Claire, they bought a semi-detached house. The other half being owned by his new in-laws. It meant they didn't often have sex in the bed because the glaring from his father-in-law slash pack alpha just wasn't worth it.

But he didn't care. He had Claire in his life. His family was safe. He had new friends, and they were out of sight, out of mind from those who would use them.

As to those Dr. Creepy claimed remained in custody? Turned out the doctor was right about one thing. They couldn't find those supposedly still being held prisoner. Without a clue, they had nowhere to start looking, but at least now the wolf packs and everyone else in the supernatural community was warned. Watching. And wary.

Despite the possible threat to their existence, Derek was happy—and learning that he got the best sex when he came home with a box of fresh treats from a pastry shop close to his work.

As for Claire...she was always moving. Always smiling. Always working on her next scheme.

"Whatcha thinking?" Derek asked, stepping outside onto the porch and wrapping his arms around his mate.

She pointed to their rather barren backyard. "We need to start a garden. I need lots of carrots. Lettuce. Cucumbers would be good, too."

"Going vegan?"

"What? Never!" she exclaimed, turning in his arms. "I noticed a family of rabbits in the field behind our place."

"You going to feed every stray you find?"

"Yes. But I'll only share my chocolate with you."

"Now I feel special."

"You should." She laughed. "I love you, Big."

"I love you more, Enny." And when people teased Derek that his wife was tougher than him, he reminded them she could beat their ass using their own arm. He even had it on video.

EPILOGUE

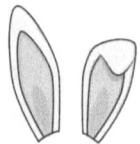

THE SCREAMING KILLED everything in a several-mile radius. Good thing Gene had conjured siren-cancelling headsets. Lana would have probably felt bad later if she'd killed all her friends.

The birth of her first child wasn't an easy one. Lana took to the water, the giant tub in her house made for two. Her mother, Bella, was on one side holding her hand, Jory on the other looking tense.

The poor man endured a lot of abuse during those few hours. Especially when it came time to push and Lana blamed him for giving their child a gigantic head.

I was kind of with her on that. Something that big shouldn't come out of a hole that small.

With much blood, cursing, and death—the insect and rodent population decimated during those cruel hours—a child was born. The screaming ended. Jory recovered—after a few slaps administered by his mother-in-law—while Lana smiled and crooned a happy song as she cradled her baby daughter.

I stood by her head and grinned like a lunatic. "She's perfect."

Neptune and the other guys were allowed to crowd into the room to stand by their respective mates. Beth still looked shell-shocked, which, given the way her hand rested on her abdomen, was for good reason. As for me, I was on the pill. No babies for me. Not yet.

Derek and I had come to the decision it was best if I had more tests run first. See exactly what kind of manipulation was done to my genes. Although, I did have to say, seeing the way Lana and Jory beamed at their green-haired daughter with the stubby wings at her back, I did feel kind of warm and mushy.

Maybe it wouldn't be so bad...

Then the baby opened her mouth and wailed.

When I stopped drooling on the floor, I revised that opinion. I also resolved to not volunteer to babysit unless my goddaughter was asleep.

Tottering on unsteady legs over to Lana, I placed a hand on her while Beth did the same on the other side.

We might have been misfits brought together by chance, but that only made our bond stronger, and our family had just gotten bigger. Together we could face anything.

Even the fact that cocoa had a bad crop year and the price of chocolate would be rising.

THE GRAINY VIDEO footage of the birth, taken via a telescopic lens from a distance, vanished, replaced by the golden icon of a lion with a spiked tail and wings.

Those at the table remained silent, waiting for the man in the suit to speak first.

"It would seem congratulations are in order for the success of our project. The child appears to be in perfect health. I see the payment to the midwife was delivered."

A woman in a white coat nodded. "The placenta has been packaged and will reach our labs before the end of the day."

"Excellent. I want regular progress on the pregnancy of the Nephilim. Do we know yet which of the subjects impregnated her?"

"No."

Not that it mattered. They'd gather samples of the new hybrid.

"What of the subject in the basement? Any change?"

"Still in a coma, sir."

Which was probably a good thing. The last time Subject Z woke, he'd tried to destroy the world.

THE END?
IF YOU KNOW ME BY NOW, THEN CHANCES ARE NO, IT'S NOT. BECAUSE WHO THE HELL IS CHAINED IN THEIR BASEMENT?!

FOR NEWS AND MORE BOOKS VISIT EVELANGLAIS.COM

www.ingramcontent.com/pod-product-compliance
Lightning Source LLC
LaVergne TN
LVHW041634060526
838200LV00040B/1571